Bird of Prey Publishing

ISBN number 978-0-9956150-0-7

# A NOTE FROM THE 'WRITER'

As my old boss used to tell me; 'Steve, you cannot polish a turd!' Now I'm not saying that my first attempt at writing is a turd. You might think so, which is fair enough. All comments are gratefully received. However, there just comes a point when you have to stop polishing!

I published this because I just had to stop. This small book has taken the best part of three years for me to write. Most of that time was spent procrastinating, working (proper jobs), sleeping, eating (lots of bad food) and drinking (too much alcohol). I'm not an alcoholic!

My other problems aside; I would like to thank my ex-boss for his very eloquent statement which helped me to just stop polishing.

# Family and Friends

Thank you family and friends for being my family and friends


Thanks for proof reading the finished book mum and Suzie

# BIRD OF PREY

By Steven Ryan

No animals were harmed in the
writing of this book!

# PROLOGUE

The seaside is a cruel and unforgiving place; build something new and it won't be long before it is destroyed by nature's unfeeling and corrosive hand. The cat had just seen the sea, in fact he'd seen the world from a completely different point of view, which included that giant body of water that he hadn't known even existed, until now. But now he was dying. He looked up at the oncoming vehicle, both his back legs shattered, he was unable to move. He felt no pain just; confusion mixed with fear. He tried to issue a meow but he could not, there was no air left in his lungs, he had taken his final breath, it was quicker this way. The car ran over him.

# CHAPTER 1

As the Watson family drove through Bexhill, travelling home to Hastings after an outing in Brighton, Mr Watson said, 'Oh Jesus, is that a cat?', 'Um, no it's probably a badger, George', Mrs Watson hurriedly replied, punching George hard in his thigh. George turned red with shame and ignored the pain in his leg.

'No! A cat - Where?' the little girl in the back seat of the car asked. She managed to push her face up against the cold glass of the back seat window just in time to see the tongue of the cat dangling from the side of its broken mouth and its collar with name tag and lots of blood and other horrible things. She screamed and fell back into her seat crying, then got up and grabbed the back of her mother's seat, 'We have to stop, we have to go back mummy!', she said, frantically shaking the seat, tears rolling down her cheeks. 'We can't darling - it's too dangerous there's so much traffic! I'm sure it felt no pain', Mrs Watson said, scowling askance at George who was still red with stupidity. She hit him three more times before they reached the traffic lights, which were not far away.

The little girl fell back into her seat again and squeezed her *Frozen Snow Glow Elsa doll* tightly into her chest, making its dress light up blue and forcing Elsa (the doll) to sing 'Let It Go'.

The little girl gritted her teeth but couldn't let it go - she thought of Flossy, her white Persian cat at home rolling around on the floor with a bag of catnip, Flossy wore a collar with a name tag too. The little girl fought to stop herself from placing Flossy at this awful scene. She failed and cried all the way to Hastings.

Don't think about it George, don't think about it! The road will clean it off the tyres by the time we get home. I hope there's none in the grille. Stop thinking about it! I'll take it to the Albanians, they only charge a fiver, they won't be bothered by bits of cat, they probably eat cat. Don't even look at the front just drop Marg and Jane off home and say I forgot to get a paper and leave it with the Albanians for half an hour. Sorted! I wonder if I've got a fiver, George thought. He never gave them a tenner because they always made out he'd given them a fiver, giving him a shrug and a free air freshener instead, which he threw away because he thought it was poisoned. He had voted Brexit and wondered if the Albanians would still be there for much longer. Are they European? He didn't know. He could have sworn the cat had fallen from the sky. Another hefty punch to the thigh snapped him from his reverie. She was bloody strong for a small woman, although she had put on some weight lately.

Two days later George had four big, black bruises on his left thigh. There would be many more bruises in the future. He would never learn. The Albanians had done a good job with the car though.

# CHAPTER 2

On a cloudless sunny, summer day in a seaside town called Bexhill-on-Sea; a town that acclaimed itself to be the home of motor racing - which was ironic considering that a lot of the cars were driven so slowly by the very rev happy and clutch slippy (although many had automatics) elderly population, which caused much anger and frustration to the younger generation of drivers - a mother seagull watched her brood of new chicks preening themselves behind the chimney stack of the 1960's bungalow, belonging to an elderly lady named Mrs Crick.

In the distance a figure appeared and began to grow in size and clarity. The figure's laughing, wagging, furry friend was straining on its lead to get somewhere that it had been a hundred times before. The bigger of the two carried a bag containing the poo of its fluffy friend which would be buried in the ground someplace with many other neatly packaged poos, or at least the ones that weren't inexplicably hung on trees or thrown on the ground. Not to mention the amount of un-bagged poos that littered the town's pavements and alleyways. Going out at night in the unlit alleys, or twittens as they were so called in East Sussex, was a lottery as to whether one would slip on the stinky substance.

The dog was looking cautiously towards the roof gable of the bungalow and as it got nearer to the birds' property began to strain less on its lead and to step more in tune with its owner and the swinging rhythm of the bag of its poo. It felt safer the nearer it could be to its master, as the mother seagull's eyes were now trained intently on them both.

The seagull didn't have many thoughts of her own which isn't to say that she was stupid. On the contrary she was actually very clever, considering the size of her brain. She could mimic the sound of rainfall by pattering on the surface of the ground with her feet, fooling earth worms and other delicacies to the surface. She could remember things and pass on behaviours to her chicks; picking up molluscs from the beach, flying up high and dropping them to smash their shells on the rocks below and following ploughs because she knew that the newly made furrow contained a plentiful supply of wriggling food. Another thing she knew was that she didn't like the approaching fluffy creature that was staring up at her with wary eyes, or its bigger counterpart. She especially didn't like the bigger counterpart. She did wonder what was in the bag though and whether it would be good to eat and how she would get hold of it but her priority wasn't the bag it was to protect her young, this was another trait passed down through generations and hard wired into her DNA. It was irrational because deep down somewhere in her very small brain she must have realised that they wouldn't attempt to scale the building, they would just pass by the same

12

way that they and many others had always done but the presence of her babies meant DNA overrode logic or reason.


The two friends were passing the house, headed toward a twitten, which was a narrow hedge-rowed and tree lined passage, the opening of which was opposite the bungalow, across the quiet road, 50 yards or so of open, uncovered ground. The dog's head rotated fully behind it, eventually looking in the complete opposite direction to which its body was travelling, he was at this moment, being dragged by the quickening pace of his owner, to the twitten that was reaching its soft gentle hands out to them, like the beckoning embrace of a mother's arms to protect them.


Halfway between the bungalow and the comfort of the twitten came the piercing high-pitched shrill as the seagull dive bombed the pair, swooping over them from behind, lifting half a dozen or so hairs on the head of the man walking his pet, shredding his nerves as he ducked low and ran into the twitten screaming, 'YOU FUCKING THING!'. The man wanted the seagull to one day come down low enough to punch the 'fucking thing' in the face. It is illegal to kill seagulls in the United Kingdom. The man wouldn't have done it anyway, either through guilt or cowardice. Most people aren't violent, especially after calm rational thought returns to them. That's what separates man from seagull. Although there are some cruel and wicked people in the

13

world, the ones who pick up their dog's poo however, don't usually fit that profile. Halfway down the twitten the man had been contemplating the seagull's murder and began to feel bad about it. The bag of recently laid faeces lay in the middle of the road, dropped during the attack. The female gull decided she didn't like what was inside the bag after sampling the contents.

This well-rehearsed and frequently played out scene was watched from the same gable by another much bigger and serene looking seagull. He was the father of the chicks and lifetime partner to the screeching, squawking woman that was currently attacking the innocent victims below. She couldn't help this behaviour because seagulls are very protective or their young. The big male knew this but didn't feel it in the same way as his partner. Seagulls are usually very caring parents. The male knew this too but didn't feel it. When the chicks were very young he would take his turn incubating their eggs, sat atop the nest in the crook between the chimney and the roof. He would take his turn to feed them as they were growing and demanding and would attend to their needs, sharing the workload equally with his partner. He knew very deep down that this is what seagulls did. He rarely followed tractors ploughing fields or mimicked the sound of falling rain, although he could comfortably do this to join in if needed. He preferred the bins along the seafront for his meals but his favourite was freshly discarded pizza crusts, he even recognised the pizza delivery mopeds and would follow them to their destination and await the remnants thrown out onto the lawns – always the crusts. He would be the first to land at the scraps where he took all he wanted and left the rest. No other bird would look at the delicious pizza crusts until he was done. Some might land nearby but they pretended to look the other way, no one approached until he was gone. He was a very big bird.

Seagulls are very bold birds, some don't even move for traffic. In quiet streets, cars would steer around them as they meandered on the roads and sometimes homeowners would come out of their front doors and be face to face with one sat on the roof of their car. The two gulls were programmed with the knowledge that a threat to their family could come from any angle and they were prepared for surprises and always stuck close to their young. Seagulls are hooligans with very little fear but the big male that lived on Mrs Crick's roof had no fear at all.

The bird and his partner were Great Black-Backed gulls and they had three chicks. Great Black-Backs will partner for life and can live into their 40s and they guard their young fiercely. Usually other birds would swoop down to take a look or grab an easy meal but this roof stayed peculiarly absent of visitors. Although gulls are largely scavengers and will eat virtually anything, they have been known to feed on young ducklings, which the big male had done on several occasions in Egerton Park, his local delicatessen. He even tried his hand at catching fully grown ducks in mid-flight but failed and largely gave up on the idea but not entirely.

The big bird could catch fish and crab from the sea, the crabs would plummet accurately from the sky onto craggy rocks. He was a hunter and had all the inherent abilities natural history had bestowed upon him but his favourite repast was pizza; maybe it was something they put in the sauce? He would spend some time on the local landfill with the thousands of other assorted gulls but mainly just to watch the commotion, basking in the atmosphere, loafing around. He didn't do much loafing since the chicks were born. He was duty bound but had a deep seated, intrinsic feeling that no harm would come to his chicks. Crows and other gulls had an in-built no fly zone around Mrs Crick's bungalow, for they also had a gut feeling; stay away from that big bird!

The sheer size of the stooped and rugged looking bird projected a physical strength, aggression and endurance to the other local wildlife around him and although he didn't know it himself, he was revered and feared by virtually everything. He'd never been in a fight before, no one would come near him, but he was imbued with a feeling of indestructability and fearlessness. He stretched his massive wings which spanned over 6 feet tip to tip, the wings that helped him, after a short run up, gain a huge amount of lift very quickly to climb into the sky. He plucked a 3 stone cod from the surface of the sea once but couldn't hold on as it writhed and fought so hard, if he'd been closer to shore he would have landed it. He held on for several minutes but couldn't grip the writhing, slippery fish. Seagulls don't have talons like birds of prey, he had a vice like grip though, but even he had his limitations and could only hold on for so long. The night the fish escaped his grasp, the bird would find half a pizza someone had discarded, he soon forgot about the big cod and carrying heavy things. He was after all, a pizza loving loafer at heart; and a murderer.

After returning from defending her babies the mother perched on the gable end staring at the mottled brown chicks that were growing at an alarming rate, they were too big for the nest now and no longer comfortably fitted on the roof, they would soon have to learn to fly and fend for themselves, but they would always be her babies. The time for them to fly was coming sooner than she thought though.

# CHAPTER 3

Mrs Crick's bungalow was semi-detached with a sweeping gable roof. At the apex of the roof stood a double chimney stack that was shared with her next door neighbour. The crook of the chimney provided shelter, a windbreak and a convenient spot to build a nest. She had an adoring cat called Mr Friedrich that she occasionally had to shoo away, when he would look lasciviously at the sparrows as they flitted in and out of her ornamental bush in the middle of the garden. She would sometimes be forced to burst into action unlocking and throwing open one of the bedroom windows in a frenzied, sweeping motion shouting at the top of her voice, 'No Mr Friedrich! No! Leave them alone!' Mr Friedrich took no notice, but the sparrows would burst from the bush, or any other conurbation that they were residing in at the time of the commotion, in rapid fire and quick slapping wings. Mr Friedrich would give up mid-stalk and sit in the middle of the lawn to lick varying parts of his anatomy as if he were just about to anyway. He was used to the game. Mrs Crick had a gardener called Martin, as her arthritis prevented her attending to the front and back gardens in the way that she would have liked. The arthritis made her a virtual hermit in the winter, only braving the cold to feed and water her beloved garden friends. She did still potter on occasion, when she could, and was so proud of both her gardens.

She revelled in watching the sparrows sprint through the air, their characters' like naughty school children, their heads bobbing up and down in the cotoneaster under the bedroom window. She loved sparrows, she thought they were like tiny flying clowns even to the point that the occasional one would fly head long into the window almost knocking itself out, although this wasn't a funny thing, she couldn't calculate the amount of pleasure they brought to her and she whiled away many an hour chuckling to herself in her clandestine observations of them; she particularly enjoyed the dust baths they would take in the flower beds on a dry summer's day, they had a favourite spot between the laburnum and forsythia which was perfect for her viewing pleasure, she watched from her spare bedroom window. Her spare bedroom was her secret bird hide. The reflection of the glass and darkness of the bedroom meant that she had a better view of the sparrows than they had of her and she would get close ups of them when they appeared to be staring into the bedroom, they were like foreign tourists, peaking through the railings at Buckingham Palace. What was behind this hard, mysterious substance that seemed to contain other birds? Sparrows can't recognise their own reflection. The tic tack of the beaks on the window made her feel part of their family. They would sometimes disappear quicker than they had emerged in a flurry of nervous energy, back into the hidden, protective depths of the bush. She could only wonder at what they got up to in the privacy of that bush, she was sure that it was more interesting and useful than what the humans got up to in their own homes; anyway what they got up to was of no matter, for Crick was the queen of sparrows in her sanctuary. She read books while sitting

19

by the magical ornithological window and when she was bored or tired of reading she would place the book on her lap and stare at her tiny friends; observing the instamatic jerks of their heads, one second they would be looking left then a millisecond later up to their right, the eye couldn't catch the movements that seemed to have no end, their busy heads and necks would never stop the exercises that saved their lives, looking out for predators or food or friends. She also loved the way the wind ruffled their feathered coats exposing the soft, fur-like, downy feathers underneath. They seemed in harmony, chirruping to each other with merry interplay and taking care of each other by using second, third and fourth sets of eyes; on a constant vigil for anything that might be missed, like Mr Friedrich. They brought her ceaseless happiness. She especially adored the fluffy younger ones and would burst with tears of joyful laughter at them but she laughed and worried about them in equal measure.


Mrs Crick loved the wildlife that visited her, including the seagulls that lived on her roof. They never bothered her, from time to time though she would hear a lot of commotion as the general public passed her bungalow. Sometimes, when she was in the garden topping up the bird seed and water, she could hear obscenities being screamed at one of the gulls. Well, why shouldn't a mother protect her family? She would think. She preferred birds to people anyway. Her home protected her from 'people' and she extended that protection, with a wall of Leylandii that surrounded the three sides of her back garden, to any wildlife that cared to visit. She would cringe and recoil whenever she saw a rat though.

As well as her favoured sparrows, Mrs Crick cherished the thrush and the black bird that were regular visitors to the assorted feeding, bathing and entertaining paraphernalia collected from her beloved *Amazon*. She loved internet shopping and Cliff Richard, especially Cliff, regardless of the vicious lies in the media about him. There was always something fishy about Rolf though so she wasn't surprised when the revelations were proved true – she was very surprised about Rolf - she was heartbroken. He always came across as a very genuine and caring man and she would cry along with him, as he cried on Animal Hospital, her favourite show from the past. Anyway the past was the past, get over it Franny! For all the hours spent watching birds through her bedroom window, Franny was not a twitcher, far from it, for she couldn't tell the sex of a bird by its colours or size and she could not name the occasional new arrival. This was therapy and she just loved to be part of; and enjoy watching the birds' simple lives.

Unfortunately Mrs Crick could not pick and choose who visited her garden; the pigeons were quick to the food she provided, 'flying rodents', who had coined that phrase? Everybody used it now and it wasn't pigeon kinds' fault that man was such a disgusting beast who wasted so much food by discarding it on

21

the street and other places which provided such a plentiful bounty for so many, so called pests, whose populations thrived and grew on it. This included the rats that came for the bird food in her fiefdom but she wouldn't admit that to herself, as the birds needed feeding. Therefore, all were welcome to her food even if some did make her shrivel in fear. It was just a shame that the pigeons were so much bigger than the thrush, black birds and sparrows but she did have to admit to herself that they actually seemed very polite most of the time, shyly making way for many of the other creatures, even the very small ones. Occasionally, if she was up early she would get to see a blanket of starlings land as one entity to clear the lawn of freshly risen earth worms and insects. The flock of starlings were like a shimmering grey and brown carpet covering the lawn, they shone and moved in one synchronistical act and would then, just as quickly as they had arrived, move on to the next bounty, which was usually breakfast on Mrs Pringle's manicured lawn next door.

In Crick's garden there seemed to be an accord or alliance between all, with only the occasional intervention required. Apart from; those dreadful magpies with their harsh disgusting staccato tones, she thought them mean and nasty, picking at the bones of other creatures, scavenging for anything, no particular preferences and no manners, even though they were probably the most intelligent visitors to her cherished garden, the only ones who could actually recognise their own reflection in a window or mirror. They also had a keener sense of self-preservation than many, such as seagulls and pigeons that looked as if they felt superior to their brethren or were they just stupid? Sometimes she time travelled when her eyes fell upon the shed nestled at the back of the garden, engulfed in Leylandii, she neglected that part of the garden now, memories from the past would flash into the present as if they were yesterday, her only grandchild, he used to hide behind that shed and she and the family would pretended they couldn't find him. Mrs Crick hadn't seen her grandson in nearly 12 years, she counted the days, although she didn't mean to. Time was a strange thing for Mrs Crick as it was for most of the people on her street who had long since retired from once busy lives, nobody seemed to know what day of the week it was anymore, every day was the same. They didn't use the Gregorian calendar anymore, rather the wheelie bin one. Everybody had three bins each, recycling was green, garden waste brown and general waste black. Nobody except for Mr Shepstone at number 12 kept track of which bins went out on what day. One day as a practical joke or as an experiment he put out the wrong coloured bin to see how many people would copy him – everybody copied him - then he brought the bin back in at midnight replacing it with the correct one. Only Mr Shepstone's rubbish was taken the next day as everyone else had put the wrong bin out. He thought it was hilarious until; that very same evening the bin men returned to collect everyone else's rubbish. The council had capitulated after the whole street had bombarded it with irate phone calls, even though it was the home owners' fault. Every household had delivered to its front door the leaflet that detailed exactly which colour bin went out on what day.

23

Shepstone was livid, 'Why are they picking up *their* fucking rubbish? If they put the wrong fucking bins out that's *their* own fault - that's more tax money wasted! They're probably getting overtime to come out again this late, the useless idiots give in too easily to all the old farts around here - they're weak! I don't know why I pay my fucking council tax!', this was aimed squarely at his wife, his vitriol was never heard by the powers that be, everything went to her, although she had noticed recently that she was becoming more and more desensitised to his rants, she basically ignored him. He never complained to the authorities or neighbours themselves or any other living soul, just the wife. Mr Shepstone was always as nice as pie to people as he met them, although his very near neighbours could occasionally hear his very loud remonstrations. That poor woman; how does she put up with him? The neighbours would gossip about them as they met in the street or while out shopping. Meanwhile the wife cared less and less about Mr Shepstone, she withdrew into her own little world and hobbies, she just about tolerated him - he had changed a lot since taking early retirement from the civil service.

# CHAPTER 4

One day as Mrs Crick was preparing her beloved cat's favourite meal – *Waitrose's special recipe organic terrine with lamb* - she became aware of a painfully high pitched screeching sound, which she had at first dismissed as someone working in their garage or another one of those stupid mopeds that buzzed around the streets all day but the sound persisted and became very meddlesome, forcing her to seek its source. She searched the house, looking in every room, it is hard to tell where a sound is coming from sometimes, she eventually realised that the sound was in the back garden and as the noise became like crystal it was clear that something was suffering. The first thing she noticed, as she peered out through the window of the back bedroom, was a circular mass of grey and white feathers spread across her lawn, as if they had all been scattered from a central core. She scanned every corner of the rectangular garden when eventually her eyes fell upon a female sparrowhawk's broad, brown flecked back and wings that were spread; like Dracula's open cloak around one his victims, the head of the bird was pecking up and down at what appeared to be a pigeon, which was living through the interminable hell of being eaten alive. Clasping her hands tightly around her ears Mrs Crick scurried back into the kitchen confused and terrified, her world was spinning and her indifference to pigeons was swapped for pity and love. The sparrowhawk, after dive bombing the unfortunate pigeon, which exploded on impact and disappeared amidst a plume of its own feathers, had hopped with its prey into a secluded corner of the pretty garden for some privacy. The rats and the magpies gathered but were well hidden and waited patiently. The big seagull atop the roof, watched on enjoying the commotion.

What must she do? Surely she must take some action? But if she ran out and shooed the bird away she'd be left with a half dead half eaten pigeon, and how would she put it out of its misery and what if the sparrowhawk took offense and turned on her to peck her eyes out or sink its talons into her skull as she ran back to the bungalow for cover? She put Cliff on the stereo, he would help gather her thoughts and soothe her shredded nerves, he had the voice of an angel that always calmed her, he was a kind and devout man and she never believed the rumours about him on the news. The screams continued behind her and they seemed to be getting louder, she cringed and began to tremble uncontrollably, that poor, poor creature! She turned Cliff up and pulled her seat closer to the speakers 'la la la- ing' out loud to 'Ocean Deep' Pull yourself together Franny! Ignoring the real world, she finally put on her headphones and turned the stereo up to full volume, tuning out the wicked world around her. Hopefully the rats and magpies would clear up the mess after the bird had finished its meal otherwise she would have to call Martin.

In-disposable Martin; he was a man for all seasons, the go to guy to get rid of all the nasty things that nature would kindly leave at Mrs Crick's door. And he did the garden too. On two separate occasions Mrs Crick had found the remains of what she was sure were mutilated ducklings. She called Martin and didn't know or care what he did with the sad remains, as long as they were gone from her realm. Many corpses would be recycled by the animals and insects at Martin's golf course where he ditched the bodies. Deep down Mrs Crick knew who the guilty party for the duckling murders was but she kept on denying it. She buried the knowledge deep and hoped that by continuing to buy him Waitrose's finest, his cruel instincts would give way to more civilised behaviour, one day. It was a vain hope.


Mrs Crick had had a happy family once, a husband and two daughters. Two were dead now, the husband and one daughter. Huntington's disease; the husband didn't know he had it until the symptoms gradually appeared and worsened, although these symptoms largely went unnoticed, mood swings and general forgetfulness, they both took the symptoms as being work related or just his age but then he started to be unsteady on his feet, he hardly ever drank but seemed drunk, slurring his words at times and the choice of words he used didn't fit in with the conversations he was having. This is when the Doctors became involved and after some time and tests; genetic testing finally revealed the diagnosis of the wicked disease. Huntington's is largely misunderstood by many of its victims, often confused with Parkinson's but Mrs Crick understood; she studied it, she knew it was an autosomal dominant mutation, she'd never heard of such terms before but she wanted to know more about the disease that was destroying her husband in front of her eyes and what to expect of it, she feared the disease and the future but the fear subsided into anger, which was good because the anger kept her going and saw her through to the end of a dreadful experience, she never hid away from it, not once. But would the emotional pain ever end? No. The disease had passed on to one of their daughters. A malicious disease which is inherited and does not skip generations, the chances of each of the daughters inheriting the disease was fifty/fifty she lost fifty percent of her family thanks to Huntington's. Manda the eldest daughter was diagnosed with the disease as was her sister's infant son. It took time but the symptoms progressed and the father and husband could no longer walk or talk or control his bladder or bowels or eventually; swallow, he'd lost his mind months ago, he was 55 when he eventually died it was long and awful for him but probably worse for those who were forced to watch and care and clean. Time is so slow when life gets bad. Mrs Crick seemed to suffer for an eternity. She didn't get to know her grandson for long, only the first three years or so of his life before his mother, the one without Huntington's, withdrew and buried herself in her career. Mrs Crick loved her grandson whom she never saw; she named her beloved cat after him. She missed her family so much.

# CHAPTER 5

This was turning out to be a good summer, a hot summer. On one particularly dry, airless day a small cat's head poked above the parapet of Mrs Crick's roof, its paws clinging for dear life to the plastic guttering, not on the hunt for seagull chicks but to see if it could jump the distance from water butt to roof – it couldn't. The kitten hugged the guttering while its hind quarters swung uncoordinatedly as it snatched the emptiness for something to grab onto. There was nothing to grab though, he knew he would have to let go eventually, as the creep of tiredness crawled all over him, he was facing a one storey free-

fall so he tried again and again to pull himself onto the roof before all his kitten energy was sapped. Before all his energy left him, reality dawned and his panic subsided as tiredness made him eventually accept his fate. Seconds before his energy failed he glanced upwards as he felt the light and warmth of the sun disappear from the top of his head, only to find himself staring into the unblinking eyes of a very big bird that had strolled down the tiled roof to investigate the kerfuffle and to meet the little black cat with the luxuriant, silky coat. The bird looked down its yellow hooked beak at the cat, seeming curious at the uninvited guest then he drew back his head and drove his dense and gnarly beak with its sharp translucent tip with an immense whipped force, between the cat's beautiful lemon yellow eyes, splitting its skull. The speed and ferocity of the attack left the beak still shiny and free of blood or brain, although an inch or so from the tip, on the underside of the bill stood a prominent feature, a blood red coloured node.

If the initial and only strike from the Black-Back didn't kill the young cat outright, the impact of the hard patio on the back of its skull meant the cat would never play the piano again. Its owners laughed so much when he would walk back and forth along the keyboard of their grand piano, making an unmelodious sound - cute and endearing. He was a lovely little cat. The notices were put through every door within a 5 mile radius of the family's home and stuck to nearly every lamp post and telegraph pole.

Mrs Crick found Mega spread eagle on his back staring sightlessly into the heavens surrounded by flies. She cried and ran tremulously back into her inner sanctum. This was before the flyers had been posted around the neighbourhood. Unable to cope, she rang Martin who came and disposed of the body by flinging it into some woods at his local golf course, as usual. Later upon seeing the flyers for the missing Mega, Mrs Crick demurred phoning the family as Martin had told her that he'd chucked the corpse somewhere at his golf course. Martin had kindly hosed and swept, with his own broom, the blood and tiny bits of brain matter from the patio. She felt it would be better if the family assumed Mega had picked a new owner. Cats do that when they find people who feed them better food. That's why she fed Mr Friedrich Waitrose's finest.

# CHAPTER 6

He didn't feel much in the way of emotions (usually) but the big bird had enjoyed the way in which Mega had hit the ground and not moved again. He wanted another go. No more cats attempted to jump onto the roof though, as he knew that they wouldn't do but as the days passed by, his mind couldn't let go of the happy feelings generated while reliving the murderous act over and over again. He looked down at Mr Friedrich stalking the sparrows' dens and ached for something new, he wasn't quite sure of what yet but the sight of Mr Friedrich made him hunger for a new adventure or past-time.

One day, after he'd tried several attempts at plucking a duck out of the sky above the park in town, he noticed a cat about the same size as Mega. Without thinking he dived at the cat which was sat preening itself in its garden, minding its own business. The act was more from frustration at missing the duck than a planned, coordinated attack. The massive bird ended the big and rapid descent by grabbing at the cat, which was sat licking the underside of its left paw at the time. The cat's shocked reaction and fear from the unexpected attack by the massive gull, which had engulfed it and turned a sunny day into a dark madness, as feathers replaced blue sky and big webbed feet clumsily groped various parts of its body, quickly switched from surprise and blind panic into vicious fury.

Instead of picking up the cat, which wasn't as small as it had seemed from the air, the bird received claws, teeth, pealing screams and furious resistance. The screaming which was unexpected, unsettled the bird and the painful injuries that the cat inflicted drove him to abandon the rash challenge and attempt to regain the safety of the sky. The massive wings pumped hard to escape the cat which had managed to sink its teeth into the bird's neck. The extra weight added by the cat made take off impossible. The sight and sound of the high-pitched and panicking seagull that was trying so hard to escape the cat's frantic grasp, for in its own panic the cat didn't know what else to do or how to react to such an unprecedented attack, would have raised nothing but disbelief. The fight ensued for at least a minute hidden away in the secluded back garden of the two up two down; a minute or 60 seconds doesn't sound like a long time but when one believes one is fighting for his life it feels like an eternity. Both felt they were fighting for their lives. Unfortunately for the bird, a cat's survival instinct is up there with the best of them and although the bird, at this moment, was blinded by panic he was also learning a very important lesson.


The faded pink legs of the gull became streaked with its own blood as the cat's superficial hold of the bird's throat let go - with a mouthful of feathers - and clawed its way down the body of the bird when the Black-Back eventually broke their connection with one last desperate, adrenalin fuelled push of its bloody feet off of the soft lawn. Finally, the ungainly movements of the wings held enough air beneath them to lift the bird away from the ground and a near death experience. The cat fell with a bump to the ground and tore through its cat flap with a pounding heart not to appear again for several days. When it did finally emerge, it no longer felt the safety of knowing it had no predators and was no longer head of the food chain, he kept a wary eye on the sky at all times. The cat was less physically scathed than the gull though as the gull's talons aren't sharp and its beak had missed a direct hit on the cat's head in all the confusion. The cat was lucky that he was only the bird's second victim because the bird would get better. For now though the bird was a mess, it would spend the next few weeks healing and studying every cat; the way they moved, the way they preened and the way they hunted prey and the way that they screamed and howled at each other to avoid a fight. While he licked his wounds he stared, he learned and he planned.

# Chapter 7

The bird reflected over the failed attack on the cat in the garden and thought about the cod he had managed to catch on one occasion from the sea. He can lift a heavy weight he knew that much but he couldn't puncture flesh with his nails. However, he could clamp his big webbed feet around things very tightly. The cat he pecked on the head was there on a plate for him, hanging defencelessly from a gutter. A frontal attack on a full grown cat whose front paws weren't preoccupied with a gutter was painful though, as cats are fast and vicious with lots of sharp things. He desperately wanted to kill another one, so he circled the neighbourhood watching cats from the safety of the sky, and over time he developed a keener eye to the shape and size of the cats on the ground and the body language they displayed; he only wanted the unsuspecting cat as he now appreciated the potency of their retaliation and the need to catch them by surprise. Cats are no fools and he was enjoying the element of risk, a sensation that he had never experienced in his life before.

One day he came across a small marmalade cat playing in a road, rolling on its back exposing its white chest and padded pink paws. He circled it. As the cat got up and walked lazily down the street he followed silently from the air. Taking his cue from his wife's attacks on the unsuspecting public he approached from the rear, swooping low, gliding inches from the ground, closing silently in on the daydreaming cat. He pulled his feet in close to his chest and honed in on the cat's head. At this point he was in autopilot and the cat's head was a crab or duckling, he felt the motion of its head and predicted with ease where it would be in time and space as the webbed feet began to extend from the undercarriage, ready to envelop and squeeze tightly around the unsuspecting feline's skull.

He felt the firmness of the domed bone and locked his strong taut webbed feet on, imagining the cod, he would not let go he squeezed with every ounce of his strength. The cat, in shock, felt like its skull was being crushed and wrenched from its body. It reacted violently but was so encumbered by the weight and momentum of the invisible object above that there was little it could do. The bird's feet did not have a perfect hold though, the right foot covered the jaw and one eye and the left held on to the cheekbone and part of the left ear which twisted the cat's head, flicking the rest of its body and the majority of its weight to the left (viewed from the rear). Being so low to the ground the bird needed to gain altitude but the cat's sudden jerky movements to one side as the seagull flapped hard trying to lift them both from the ground meant that its right wing crashed into the ground on its powerful down-stroke. He managed to gain three or four feet which brought the cat airbourne but the bird realised quickly that he was running out of street and knew that if he didn't release his cargo he would crash into the living room window of the forth coming bungalow. He let go and soared as the weight was released.

The cat, with its uncovered eye, could see the rapidly approaching bungalow too but at this point was in a state of dazed confusion from its awareness of losing touch with terra firma and becoming weightless, before it could make any sense of its predicament though, the cat began tumbling across the lawn of the bungalow, the tight, pink helmet released from its head. The cat ended up on its back looking skyward at a disappearing bird with a mix of relief and abject bewilderment, if the cat were human it would have been patting itself down, checking for broken bones but this cat knew instinctively that it he was okay so he just laid there for a minute or two looking to the heavens as he came down from his high.

The bird didn't give up he tried several more times, picking longer streets or fields. All the elements had to be right. Perfecting his craft made him feel good, he'd never felt this before. He had practised all his skills as a youngster but could not remember the gratification of getting something right, or wrong, as far as he was concerned he had always been perfect. Except at pulling grown ducks from the sky, he wasn't thinking about ducks anymore.

He always dropped the cats if he didn't catch them just right; by gaining a firm hold with his middle digit at the bottom rear edge of the masseter (a thick powerful muscle that closes the cat's mouth) the rest of his large webbed feet would naturally

37

envelop the muscle for a good solid purchase which gave the added bonus of forcing the cat's mouth shut. The discordant tones of a screaming cat rankled so. It took one big coordinated effort but he got better and better until; he rode the thermals in ascending circles realising that he flew as if unburdened with a 1 stone passenger. He also realised that he was beginning to enjoy the rush he got from catching the cat by surprise and not knowing if his ever strengthening wings would break the stubborn grip of gravity, for that tremendous thrust which was needed to break the bond between cat and pavement. The thrashing and twisting didn't help his grip but the technique was improving with practice.


He had mastered the silent snatch but there was still the element of danger because once locked on it was difficult to let go, especially when focussing every neuron and muscle fibre to the take-off, knowing that if the cat was too heavy he could end up rectrices (tail feathers) over beak in a bush or bungalow wall which would hurt and expose him to possible attack. Usually after a few minutes the cat would stop thrashing around and enter a kind of trance-like state, noticing the world from a different perspective, they would relax and enjoy the ride but the ones that didn't enjoy the ride would thrash constantly and the bird needed to get where he was going quickly before the head slipped the noose.

# CHAPTER 8

When the bird took the cats up into the sky and dropped them he would look down as they tumbled around in the air, most would somehow manage to right themselves, landing on their feet. The cats sustained many types of injuries such as broken legs and bodies and death, depending on the height he dropped them from and what they landed on. He dropped some in the sea and then landed next to them as they frantically paddled aimlessly around looking for land, with terror stricken faces. He bobbed up and down and dipped his head under the surface of the water to watch them disappear, twisting and turning into the murky darkness until all he could see and feel was the last tiny bubbles escaping from their water logged lungs.

His favourite site of disposal though was King Offa Way, a busy bypass that when viewed from the air cut a long grey path through the ever expanding seaside town. He liked it here because it was a big target with fast moving cars that would obliterate the cat just after impact, if dropped at exactly the right time. Sometimes he would land on the foot bridge that spanned the bypass to watch the carnage. He always aimed the cats just past the bridge so he could get a good look. He didn't laugh but sometimes he'd peel a raucous caw which was drowned out by the traffic mayhem beneath him

Motorists predominantly reacted by attempting to steer around the stricken, dead or wounded felines but inevitably the animals would be hit as the cars swerved and straddled the white lines and back again to avoid colliding with each other. Some cats popped as their internals entered the external world like ripe, squeezed zits, accompanied by the crunching sound of splintering bones. The occupants of the cars could feel the bump as they rode over the body and cringed or cried or laughed.

From the trees and hedges that edged the dual carriageway came a harsh clacking sound like football rattles. Then the heads of the chattering scavengers would emerge through the foliage to see the new feast. They were drawn by the commotion and then the smell of fresh blood and guts warming up on the hot tarmac under the midday sun. The beautiful birds with the iridescent shine to their coats that turned metallic blue to black and back to blue with every change of direction, hopped in and out of the road, dodging the traffic, to peck at the food so thoughtfully provided by the giant seagull, while all the time issuing their sadistic cries. People or cultures give each species a score or value to its life, cats get a high score in England, magpies nowhere near so high but they are blissfully unaware of this, to them cats taste as good as any other meat, including their own. Their blood curdling cries challenge all other creatures who so revile them for their arrogance. They are keen and clever scavengers and sometimes killers and this particular spot would become a favourite of theirs, as many more easy meals would soon present themselves, free-falling from the sky.

Surprisingly the smeared cat bodies were never accompanied by dead magpie.

# CHAPTER 9

Thousands of cars pass under the bridge on King Offa Way on a daily basis, people are usually in a hurry to get somewhere. Not all people but most wouldn't deliberately run a cat over and if they did would probably feel bad for several days afterwards. Very few would stop though, preferring a guilty feeling for a while, rather than to check whether the cat had survived the ordeal, the majority would just carry on their way. Some people who owned cats thought about stopping, but the road was too fast and dangerous to stop. However, the mounting number of cat deaths in that area did not go unnoticed, not only by the street cleaners and magpies but by many very concerned cat loving members of the public.

Along with the increasing number of complaints to the council, which were all forwarded to the transport, roads and parking (dead animals) department, there were also reports of drowned cats washing up on the beach along the coastline of Bexhill. The local *Onlooker* newspaper was quickly onto the phenomenon, publishing the locals' ideas on the causes to the abundance of cat corpses in the area. Apart from those who: conjectured that the cats were being abducted by aliens and discarded after their experiments or the theories on the widening spread of cat depression similar to the increasingly prevalent depression among human society which concluded by the unfortunate cats taking their own lives – for there is not the kind of support and understanding for cat depression as there is for human depression; or increasing $CO_2$ emissions and the impending end of the world which was affecting the cats' intuitive ability for self-preservation, making them accident prone around that particular bridge, possibly due to the pollution from all the traffic, the change in brain chemistry  caused by the pollution making the cats dizzy could have been giving the cats a misbelief that they could swim to France for a baguette. Overall though; the animal loving readers' opinions were united by outrage and an outpouring of grief and emotion at the fact that nothing was being done to track down the swine/s who were spree killing the innocent moggies, and the weight of public concern demanded action. It was a good story and the paper could see lots of traction in harassing the local politicians and ridiculing the police who seemed to be doing nothing about it. The police *were* doing nothing about it.

The good-publicity hungry politicians happily sympathised with the public concern. Councillor, Lord Anvil was quoted as saying; 'I have 2 cats of my own who are part of my family, it would break our hearts if anything happened to them, of course we will do everything in our power to stop this heinous crime and find who is doing this awful thing. I will make it my personal responsibility to coordinate with the District Commander of Rother police to catch whoever it is and bring them to justice and stop this awful crime'. He didn't have any cats, which the paper later found out from one of the councillor's 'friends' or neighbours, they delighted in exposing him.  More people complained about the number of potholes in the roads than about the dead cats but it was good front page stuff and papers love to align and ingratiate themselves to certain groups of society, when the time is right, and take up a cause when it sells more papers. They had a great front page picture of a wet, dishevelled Ginger moggy lying spread eagle on the pebbles of Bexhill seafront, the waves lapping at its feet but the picture was taken from a tasteful distance so the details were slightly indiscernible, but still evocative. 'What's happening to our cats?' read the headline with; 'We want answers! Bla bla bla...' People posted on the paper's website their disgust and fear at the deaths and one said that the cat shouldn't have gone swimming when the red flags were out, it was its own damn fault!

From local to national to international the mystery story spread, shining a light on the town. It was good for business, Bexhill was becoming famous.

# CHAPTER 10

The police weren't really interested in dead cats, apart from those police officers who owned cats themselves, but as an organisation paid for by the taxpayer they had a responsibility to respond to calls from the increasing number of tax and non-taxpayers who were complaining that nothing was being done about the hideous crimes. The majority of the general public naturally assumed there was a human behind the cat killings and he, she or they needed to be tracked down and punished as soon as possible. The impression generated and fuelled by the press was that the public wanted at least one head for the crime. However, the reality was that even if it were a human committing the crimes, and they were caught, he, she or they would probably just be fined and banned from owning cats for three months, as is the kind of punishment meted out to cruel people who inflict pain on animals in the UK. British justice would never see the killer thrown from the bridge or drowned, there was no eye for an eye in this country's justice system but if the animal rights people got the bastard they would surely hang him.

The police would logically, have loved to catch the perpetrator of the crimes even though they were snowed under with other (higher priority) cases. For example, an arsonist burning down flats with people still inside them and the small matter of the foreign student nearly kicked to death in broad daylight, while walking along Bexhill's glorious seafront, by a gang of youths. As the pressure mounted via the local rag and despairing voices from local and global animal charities and Facebook upon the council, so in turn did the pressure escalate upon the police.

The Divisional Commander, Pete Stevens, felt this pressure most. He didn't have a cat or really give a damn about animals in general. He cared more about people being beaten in the street for no apparent reason and arsonists burning down homes. He had interviews with the Regional TV stations, not through choice but by order of the District Commander who'd had an earful from Lord Anvil at the last Mason's meeting, the District Commander was a rare female member at the Masons, of this she was proud although it was just another means to an end, she had broken many moulds during her sprint up through the ranks, almost writing her own rule book, she was inspirational to women officers in the county who were now firmly accepted as part of the fabric of the institution and were beginning to make great strides forward, attaining higher and higher posts. It was this District Commander and women like her who paved their way to more successes. She revelled in the prestige, but Anvil after having been exposed as a liar and ridiculed by the *Onlooker,* was desperate to salvage some pride and the District Commander owed Anvil big time for certain 'favours' over the years that yielded her lofty status and salary and enormous pension, that she planned to cash in at the ripe old age of 55, but at what cost to her personal life? The Commander wasn't the sharpest tool in the box but she was no fool and had enough charm and charisma to carry off her role in style, the role was mainly delegation, signing bits of paper in a big office, the hours were long and draining and the pressures severe, she worked nearly every hour god sent, if the big salary she claimed was divided by the number of hours she actually worked, she probably earned less than a shelf stacker in *Tesco*, but she was proud of her achievements, the single-minded woman suffered for her achievements by way of the cost in time to herself and her family, she never went home. She dismissed the occasional pangs of guilt over her family and ignored an inner turmoil of a mother who had, at some point, reached a fork in the road and had to make a choice between family and career, it was an easy choice at the time. She liked her wine too which took her to a place outside of what was her 'real life' until she was ready for work again the next day, she didn't really know what a 'real life' was anymore but deep down she craved an ordinary one. The wine and the work helped to keep those deep down cravings in check and silenced the inner voice while she continued her march away from mediocrity or towards something better. Now The District Commander delegated down the chain of command to Pete Stevens who followed orders, but whose scruples would not give the cats priority over people, he put on a brave and sympathetic face for the press and lied that his best people were on the case.

# CHAPTER 11

The big eyes staring up pleadingly, the fur in slow motion - swirling from side to side, and the up stretching paws reaching for what – Oxygen, land and hope? The bird's eyes watched the last air bubble escaping the left nostril, he pushed his head deeper under to keep the sinking white Persian in view for as long as possible through the murk and grime, then he took a drink, all the flying and carrying that extra weight demanded rehydration, and although he preferred fresh water, he could drink the sea and excrete the salt through his eyelids. He was a clever bird and used everything his ancestors had bestowed upon him from evolution. He fancied diving down and grabbing the cat by the face so he could bring it back up to the surface again, to watch it sink for a second time, but he'd done this before and was captured in the clutches of two desperate paws with sharp protracted claws and was nearly dragged down by the weight of the desperate, tired and dying creature. He escaped but it was another close brush with death and he was learning quickly from his mistakes. When he dropped them in the water he would land, bobbing up and down, not too far away from them, so that they would swim to him as the nearest buoyant thing around to grab hold of, he always moved just enough, so he was just out of their reach, until they were worn out and began taking big gulps of sea. He was such a tease. With their energy depleted the cats would try to breathe the water and sink. It kept him occupied. He always picked light coloured cats to drop in the sea because he could keep sight of them for longer in the grubby water.


The local cats weren't happy, they'd noticed their numbers dwindling and even the ones that hadn't been attacked had an eerie instinct to keep looking over their shoulders for something to fear, they didn't know of what to fear for exactly but they were scared. The minor reduction in the cat population made the sparrows happy, and they would have felt it was a good thing for the cats to finally get a taste of their own medicine. The sparrows had a growing sense of more space and freedom, old habits die hard though and their compulsion to look for predators carried on, their little heads moved just as quickly as they ever had. The sparrowhawk which seemed to catch more pigeons than sparrows didn't notice any change, she could pluck other birds from the sky easily and she did this frequently by dive bombing them from above, she considered taking seagulls sometimes but never did, on one occasion she even looked at the black-back from above but when she'd closed in had noticed a cat hanging from beneath it, she did a double take and then a small brown mouse in a freshly cropped field over a mile away took her attention. The big seagull looked her casually in the eye before the streamline killing machine swept away to collect the snack that foraged unsuspectingly in the distant field.

The seagull couldn't count but he appreciated quantity and he'd finished off quite a few cats. Killing cats was like pizza crusts; sometimes there were just not enough but other times there were too many and he would have to leave the some to the other scavengers. He hadn't had enough of this diet yet, in fact, his appetite was getting bigger by the day which meant that the other scavengers, who sometimes benefitted from the leftover pizzas, were doing alright too.

# CHAPTER 12

A skinny Abyssinian (cat) called Joseph (named after Joseph and the amazing Technicolor dreamcoat) raced along the top of narrow wooden fences, wide walls and across low roofs keeping one eye fixed on the limp hanging body of a flying cat and the other eye on the obstacles he was traversing. If Joseph was a car he'd be a pearlescent Formula One racing machine, his coat was milky blue with bands of slate grey and he appeared to change from glimmering blue to grey with every movement and change of sunlight upon his lean, muscular body. He was very fast, very beautiful and very clever. He didn't seek the limelight but when people saw him, most stopped to admire him. He wasn't vain, even though he knew he drew a lot of adoring attention from the humans. His most compelling and overriding trait was his inquisitiveness and currently, chasing this new wonder, had his complete attention. The chase ended on the footbridge crossing King Offa Way, where he stopped and sat down with head up to the sky watching the black wings in the distance, circling like a jumbo jet waiting for the runway at Gatwick to clear. The bird was actually circling upwards as he was under an enormous but lonely, desolate cloud that was conveniently resting directly over his target zone, the cloud's thermals were lifting the bird to greater heights with little or no effort from the bird himself needed. He was enjoying the free ride, unaware of his audience on the bridge beneath.

The jumbo was looking to drop its meaty cargo in the right place or on second thoughts, head south a few hundred yards and watch it drown in the sea. The jumbo's feet were aching though and it was in just the right spot as the traffic lights at the westerly end of King Offa Way had turned green and a tidal surge of metal boxes headed en masse towards the footbridge. He instinctively let go. Joseph's head followed the tumbling object in the sky upon its descent and the closer it came, what started out as a sound muffled by traffic noise, crystallised into piercing screams, until the cat passed out of his sight beneath the footbridge, followed by a dull but perceptible thunk. The screams were replaced by horns and bumper cars. The cars flicked from lane to lane trying their best to avoid the body in the road, Joseph meandered to the bridge's edge where the cat had fallen and stuck his head through the railings to look down upon the chaos. Nothing to see, so he meandered to the other side of the bridge, stuck his head through the railings and looked down. There wasn't much left of the unfortunate cat apart from a wide, reddish-brown, shimmering streak in the shape of a giant letter S, which started from the outside lane and crossed over the carriageway to the inside lane. The cat's head was intact facing upwards on the central reservation so Joseph, if in any doubt, had confirmation of what it was he had tracked from the sky.

Joseph's fascination and concentration was absolute as he took in the carnage beneath and before him, so much so that he hadn't noticed the black shadow across the carriage way and the disappearance of the warmth from the beating sun on the back of his head. His sharp cat instinct told him to look up and when he was looking fully up, head still through the balustrade of the footbridge, he was staring directly into the unblinking eyes of a downward facing seagull which was perched on the railing directly above him. Just like the bird, Joseph didn't know fear and as he looked up, his mind was still in its observational and bemused, curiosity mode. It's an unusual story even for a cat to work out and 2+2 didn't necessarily equate to 4 in this case. Some parts of the jigsaw take a while to slip into place and he didn't suspect or feel any threat from the giant bird above him at this moment.

The magpies were a bit pissed off because the major chunks of the just flattened, crushed and pureed cat were in the middle of the carriageway and they liked the mess to be on the edge of the outside lane for health and safety reasons. Between traffic light changes though, they managed to get most of the gourmet jelly which they celebrated with their chorus of machinegun-like yells.

The giant bird couldn't have attacked Joseph even if he'd wanted to and he did want to. He'd already figured he could carry the skinny cat quite easily but not from a standing start and not from below the railing of a footbridge, so if he did ever exude a threat he wasn't exuding it now and Joseph was well aware of this by virtue of his innate catty instincts, which were keener than any other cat's, this side of East Sussex at least. So they just stared at each other, for quite some time, thinking, not sure of what exactly but just their lizard brains filtering the noise and calculating permutations in the background. Although he didn't realise it at the time, the bird had no idea that this was not a potential prey but the spectre of his own grisly demise.

# CHAPTER 13

Parts of the jigsaw did fall into place that night as Joseph was having his belly rubbed by his adoring 7 year old human, after a particularly delicious jellified meal of salmon, chive and grape (gourmet of course). He wasn't one for pampering as he preferred to explore and discover but he loved his little owner, or part owner, and allowed her the pleasure of rubbing his belly, on occasion. On this occasion the belly rub brought an epiphany. The bird killed the cat at the bridge furthermore the bird had killed more cats, many cats. He didn't know it, or notice it at the time, but cats were disappearing and one in particular, his next door neighbour who he hadn't thought much about, until now. He'd gone! And as he'd walked the mean streets of Bexhill-on-Sea there were less and less cats around, which he actually liked, but he was now quickly coming to realise, as the little hand moved from chest to navel for the 15$^{th}$ time, was a bit disconcerting (the cats disappearing, not the hand). He missed his feline brethren even though he didn't really like them. He hated the way he purred uncontrollably, he liked to be in control but his mind was crystal clear when in a state of pure relaxation and while he digested the salmon and released his midriff to the owner that he trusted implicitly he thought and purred, and the thoughts took form, and the more he purred 2+2 began to equal 4, the pieces of the jigsaw were falling into place.

Cats don't talk but they do communicate with each other: posture (ears, eyes, tails and smiles), different sounds and smells. Joseph was a master of all the units that made up the language of the universe, especially the language between himself and his own kind, hence in his 7 years he'd never been in a fight or altercation and he would never back down or runaway. All matters were dealt with by diplomacy – he always got his own way.

As part of his thinking process Joseph would sidle through the ornaments around the house knocking the odd one or two to the ground as he sniffed and rubbed them for texture and feel. He didn't think with his brain alone, he used his whole body and experience and sometimes the family endured collateral damage but he could not help this as he was very inquisitive and needed to experience things first hand and not by sight alone. He didn't always trust what he saw.

He needed to find this bird and learn its habits. He needed the cats to unite. Then he would have another belly rub and put all the parts together. Note to self; don't get dropped on tarmac from a great height by a very big bird! This was the real reason that he needed to bring about the end to the bird's fun.

# CHAPTER 14

Most people turn up to work every day to get paid so that they can afford to follow their pursuits outside of work, not for the love of the job. Some jobs are vocations that people love and are fulfilled by. Regardless of the job role: some people are good at what they do, bad at what they do, somewhere in the middle or just completely indifferent. This includes doctors, lawyers, barmen, road sweepers and the police. The police do have a few bad ones and Bexhill in particular had two really bad ones in PC Wilkin, a delicate little man, and PC Franklin a petite female with the heart of a lion and the brain of a chimpanzee, the police gradually removed height and intellectual restrictions for recruits in the early 90's, as less and less people wanted to join the 'force'. Franklin, who looked better in her uniform than in her civvies, was a mousy, unexceptional looking woman, like a female version of PC Wilkin. PC Wilkin had slightly effete features which included a lacklustre chin and small piggy, button nose and was slightly bug eyed due to a problem with his thyroid which made him look like a toad face 'Wilkins you fucking ugly c***, you look like a toad', 'lol', Wilkin loved bants (banter) with his colleagues - he didn't actually and he was a very sensitive soul deep down. Unfortunately for Wilkin the thyroid problem had been noticed during the three day course on the use of a Taser which didn't just tackle the operation of the machine itself but also when to use it, almost a fifth of the attendees to the course failed, but he'd failed on medical grounds which galled him and he felt slightly jealous that Franklin had passed the tests and now wore one of the garish yellow objects, proudly on her bat belt. Standards in the UK have unfortunately declined consistently since the war and these were two unremarkable people who scraped through their training. Evolution tries to extinguish the weak but a small percentage of the human race evolved a very big brain and a conscience, which prolonged and protected the weird, wonderful and the useless. These two, as well as, a large swathe of British society were unwitting recipients of science's advances and protection and public generosity.

One of PC Wilkin's most embarrassing incidences took place on Bexhill Town Hall Square where one solitary (half empty at the time of the incident) pub stood, there were three police vans placed strategically around the square, including one with 'smile you're on CCTV' emblazoned all over its bright yellow bodywork. There were more police in and around the square than there were patrons inside the pub. But this was a deterrent, according to the police, which worked in reducing alcohol related crime. Every police person was dressed in black and wore stab-proof vests (which made them look bigger) with various ancillaries attached that made them feel safer but to appear even more intimidating to the general public, the real criminals were not bothered by the paraphernalia because they knew their rights. Since the recession and many years of borrowing, the public sector gravy train was becoming mired in thick and lumpy gravy, 'cut backs', 'we all need to tighten our belts', say the poor politicians. The train will stop arriving at the station soon enough. So why so many policepersons at Town Hall square that night? The Divisional Commander, Pete Stevens had a budget like many others and needed to use up those funds for fear of receiving less the following financial year. The government were currently fighting on all fronts in particular against public sector strike after public sector strike, as they tried to revoke decades of perks and promises, the workers were being squeezed; like a cat's head under a heavy Volvo. However, The Divisional Commander, Pete Stevens' gravy, although noticeably thicker these days, was still smooth enough to enable him to hand out the overtime, which was a good way to use up his allotted funds, so that he could get the same again, or near to it, next year. That's why all departments of government are so good at statistics. Yes there was a recession and everyone, except the politicians, had to tighten their belts but the police had an ace up their sleeves; terrorism, with the increasing number of terror attacks around the world, especially in the new post Brexit Europe, would the Europeans have our backs? These were uncertain times with unanswerable questions and it put the fear, of many different gods of all types of persuasions, up Joe public and the politicians alike. Politics aside, there were a lot of police hanging around Town Hall Square that night and the police had money, pepper spray and Tasers.


A man who was on a night out with a friend had just had two pints of beer in the Town Hall Square pub and was standing outside the half empty pub waiting for his friend to take a pee. PC Wilkin approached the gentlemen on the empty pavement from behind and with all the authority he could muster, squeaked; 'Move on' to the gentleman waiting for his friend. 'No I'm waiting for a friend, who's in the toilet, in this pub', 'Don't argue with me, I said move!', 'No', 'Look, I said don't argue with me, I'm telling you to move on right now!', 'and I said no, I am waiting for my friend!', 'how much have you had to drink?', 'two pints, we've only been out an hour for Christ's sake!', 'do you want to get in the car?', PC Wilkin pointed to the police car across the road. 'Yeah, fine', said the man who was getting more and more irritated but was just about managing to keep his temper in check, as the two pints of self-righteous indignation began flowing faster through his arteries and veins. He felt his fists clenching and released them quickly. 'Put me in the car' the man said, 'Look just do as I say, move on and there doesn't have to be any trouble', PC Wilkin was agitated and nervous as the natural assumption when a 'normal' person is instructed by someone in a stab-proof vest and a radio and pepper spray and whatever else he had hanging from his bat-belt, no Taser, while surrounded by 30 other similarly attired gestapo would be: 'yes sir', he didn't expect the response he received and really didn't want to put a man in 'the car' for standing outside a pub but had passed the point of no return by now, he was just testing his super powers on the public after all. Just at that moment PC Franklin joined in the altercation like a Jack Russell yapping at their heels, 'you heard him, move on or you'll get in the car!', 'Put me in the car, I haven't done anything wrong, I'm standing by a pub in an empty street waiting for my mate to have a piss!'. By this time a small crowd had gathered and as Wilkin and Franklin ushered the man to the car holding his hands behind his

60

back the man shouted; 'OUCH Police brutality!', 'shut up! I'm barely touching you' said Wilkin, who was barely touching the man but was nervous and becoming very jumpy. Franklin wasn't though, she was in full flow shouting at the criminal, 'Shut up he's barely touching you, if you'd done as you were told you wouldn't be in this situation, you've only got yourself to blame', 'I haven't done anything!'


In the car the vicious swine who was standing outside the pub in Town Hall Square was given another chance to redeem himself, by which time his mate who had driven down from Tunbridge Wells for a night out in the Vegas of the south of England had finished with the toilet and was back outside in time to see his friend being bundled into the police car, Wilkin kindly placed his hand on the felon's head so he didn't knock it on the roof of the car. The friend approached Franklin, who was hopping from one foot to the other outside the car to keep an eye on the baddie, to find out what was going on. Franklin filled in the mortified friend and told him that if his friend didn't see sense very quickly he'd be taken to Hastings and put in a cell. Inside the car Wilkin said 'Listen, all you need to do is admit that you were in the wrong and apologise and you can go with a verbal warning', 'you must be joking', 'I am not joking, just apologise and you can go on your way', 'are you joking? All I was doing was standing outside a pub', the two pints of righteous indignation had reached its pinnacle and the stubbornness, bitterness and anger had set to intractable resistance. There was a tap on the window from the man's friend, 'Steve, just apologise and let's get out of here!', 'I haven't done anything wrong!', 'just do what they want mate.'

'Do you want to get in the van?' Wilkin's last play, surely Steve would see sense, even his mate was telling him to apologise, no way would he get in the van; 'Yeah put me in the van', the righteous indignation problem had plagued Steve his whole life, even when sober, he carried the weight of the world on his shoulders and was as stubborn as a mule but with two pints in him he became a cantankerous twat but for some inexplicable reason managed to contain most of his anger on this occasion, to an extent. They ended up doing a dance in the back of the van because Steve wouldn't sit next to Wilkin who eventually knelt on Steve's back to put the handcuffs on. 'You have to sit next to me' said Wilkin 'up yours!' said Steve.

Steve ended up in a cell and his mate's mum had to drive down from Tunbridge Wells at 1 o'clock in the morning with the spare keys to his car, as his were locked in Steve's flat. Steve's anger lasted the whole night plus a few weeks and months; he'd had his finger prints and a DNA sample taken and spent the rest of his life hating the police.

Desk Sergeant: 'Are you fucking joking! You brought someone who was standing outside a fucking pub in Bexhill, in a van to

Hastings? You stupid little c***! And it was captured on CCTV by our own fucking van across the street'. The Sergeant had backed Wilkin up, he had no choice, but the situation was embarrassing. As it turned out the threats Steve was; not shouting, but expressing in a very loud voice about telling the press and getting a solicitor, even requesting a pen and paper to record the whole incident (he'd forgotten about the CCTV van) on the advice of the duty solicitor, who also told him to be careful and keep his voice down, came to nothing. The incident only slightly dented PC Wilkin's impetuosity and self-belief, as the mighty organisation and brotherhood behind him imbued him with a sense of imperviousness. He quickly moved on from the incident but never stopped being a dick.


Some people are just dicks and some people are just bad at their job. Wilkin was both and so was Franklin. Franklin would be promoted later for her role in capturing the cat killer and from then on she moved swiftly up the chain of command with only one or two minor setbacks on the way, eventually becoming a police commissioner, it helped that she was a woman in this period of history, as the police stringently practiced a positive discrimination policy but this in turn meant that Wilkin, who would later become her husband, also benefitted from the meteoric rise with a variety of promotions of his own. The pair was ridiculed for their incompetence by their sub-ordinates but neither really noticed and didn't catch the sarcasm in remarks that came from all directions. They were blessed with ignorance. They were a perfect complement to each other.

63

Present: Wilkin and Franklin were assigned the cat murder case even though they were not currently part of CID. The CID was busy with real crimes and Wilkin and Franklin were told to get into plain clothes and catch the murderer. They were promised promotions if they could get to the bottom of it quickly and catch someone. Steven's, the Divisional Commander, was confident that they wouldn't catch the felon but he'd fulfilled his obligation to the District Commander and put two of his best people on it and the press duly reported to the concerned public of the police's new commitment and effort to capture the sadist, which relieved some of the pressure, for the time being.

# CHAPTER 15

Three kids were up an old oak tree next to a footbridge that traversed King Offa Way. The footbridge passed over to Bexhill old town. But the side they were on sat next to a retirement home with big windows and some balconies over-looking a narrow band of foliage (including the tree the kids were in) and a footpath that led downhill in an easterly direction on their side and adjacent to the road.

The kids were trying to capture someone in their death throws, to post online. They had a morbid website that celebrated the macabre called death-row.uk, a euphemism for Bexhill and for this street in particular which had twentyish retirement homes on it – it was actually called Hastings road, which had been cut in two by King Offa Way and then joined up again via a footbridge. The black 'private' ambulances were regular visitors to Hastings road. In actual fact, Bexhill was more like an elephants' graveyard than a death-row, as people chose to move there in their dotage. Not that Bexhill was without its unsavoury element, some of whom should have been on the real life death-rows (none of which are in the UK) but Bexhill wasn't as bad as the young locals made it out to be. It was a good place to come and die but like most teenagers they were bored and would rather live in London, which wasn't that far away but took ages on the train, when the trains weren't on strike. At least they weren't sat in front of a PlayStation all day killing zombies and were getting in touch with nature by hanging in trees. Ironically, Hastings road's pavements were on a deep camber with jagged paving slabs and pot holed tarmac, any old biddy pushing her near-death fella in a wheel chair would struggle to move him along it, most ended up in the road itself. One day a private ambulance, in a hurry, knocked a married couple, of over 60 years, over. A broken hip in an 80 plus year old can be fatal, she ended up in the same black ambulance, delivered free of charge to the morgue at the Conquest hospital.

Mike: 'Seriously Karl, we can only see in one room and he's sitting up eating steak and kidney pie', 'How do you know its steak and kidney?' Freddy, 'Fuck off you dick it's a fucking pie! Whatever it is, he's not about to peg it, this was a bad idea, we can't see a fucking thing and I'm not sitting here all day, we'd be better off down the seafront waiting for someone to have a stroke or a heart attack. Do we seriously want to see someone die? The site's shit anyway – no one looks at it'. The kids were all 14 years old, nearly 15.

The old man glanced over his shoulder and saw three kids dropping out of a tree, just a few yards from his window, and then resumed the consumption of his delicious steak and kidney pie. Karl was the clever one, Mike was a gangly 6ft and only ever wore white, which could look cool, or not, depending on one's fashion point of view but he did okay with the chicks, regardless of his greasy spotty face. He didn't care about the spots so didn't come across as self-conscious. He wasn't self-conscious, which made him very cool and very confident but not arrogant. Not as cool as Mike though who wore a hat and was intellectually clever and switched on in a world savvy way too. And then there was Freddy.

The whole enterprise was Karl's idea and the other two just followed, they weren't great thinkers. Karl was generally bored which kept him busy and the other two just dragged along behind as they had done for many years because they had little imagination or ideas of their own, although they would start to think for themselves soon. They'd probably sleep all day if it were not for their luck of meeting Karl on their first day of secondary school. They had their uses to Karl so he was happy that they tagged along.

Mike's whites were stained green and brown from rolling down the embankment to the road, he looked like a bad National Trust signpost. He didn't care though, which is pretty cool in and of itself but selfish people seem unaware of the world about them or what others think, they go through life without a care in the world, and why should they care? The world doesn't. Freddy, when not with his mates, watched internet porn all day. His brain was physically smaller than the other two's, who weren't averse to a bit of internet porn now and then but weren't obsessed in the same way as Freddy. Karl had watched a YouTube video about internet porn once, which suggested something about mirror neurons in the brain which enslave you to the image on the screen, usually of complete freaks inflicting pain on each other and making the most unnatural noises, and when the subject sought relief (Freddy) he'd release pleasure chemicals like dopamine, an addictive agent that acts as a reward. Anyway, it went on to say that a person would become desensitised and needed more and more stimulation of this dopamine rush. The whole video basically led to the conclusion that people obsessed with internet porn developed smaller brains and Karl suspected Freddy had a small brain and was well aware of his constant frustration and anger. Karl was no psychologist but he'd watched plenty of Ted-Ed videos so he knew enough. Basically internet porn fucks with the wiring and Freddy's wiring was definitely fucked. Freddy also agreed to everything Karl suggested which was good for Karl and kept his hands clean, not that Karl was a super villain or anything, just a bit cautious. Freddy would never get the time he deserved, to develop a meaningful relationship that might, in time, have increased the size of his disproportionately small porn brain.

As the boys regained their composure on the bank Freddy suddenly hollered, 'There must be 200 cats!' There were 503 cats to be precise, on the bridge, staring directly upwards into the fluffy clouded, Azure coloured sky, their heads circling as they pursued the courier of death in the sky. Some were standing, but most sat patiently and calmly, just looking up at the sky without expectation. 'Fuck! Are they hypnotised? I'm feeling a bit freaked out. Maybe we're on T.V. look for cameras - It could be like, some Derren Brown shiii!' Before Freddy could finish his sentence the cats' heads had stopped swaying and every agile body tensed with anticipation, the ones that sat were now standing in a fixed rigid stance like statues, the light breeze moving the fur atop the hard unmoving bodies. The boys thought they could feel the vibration from the simultaneous contraction of the muscles in 503 cats as they flicked to red alert, as if about to jump on an unsuspecting mouse that poked its head out of a hole in the skirting board. The heads were now moving slowly down from the sky toward one side of the bridge. Then an explosion of movement; the cats surged, as if becoming one single entity, towards the barrier as if committing mass hara-kiri, heads clattering through the upright aluminium bars. 503 heads pushed through approximately 80 feet in length of railing many were scrambling on top of others. The ones at the bottom of the pile were oblivious of the clambering paws on their backs, all they wanted was a view of the tumbling body, which was about to meet terra-firma with a deplorable crunch. The peculiar view from the road heading east was that the entire length of the bridge had been decorated with furry faced totem poles. Some heads were piled 5 or 6 deep, which was confusing enough until a cat bounced off of the tarmac in front of the oncoming traffic. It actually bounced, causing the two lead cars that were neck and neck to brake hard. The speed camera was on the other side of the road (westbound) so cars would race up the eastbound side doing way over the 40 mph speed limit and in the split second it took for the cat to land on the road and

69

bounce, the drivers' surprise meant that they couldn't decide which lane to be in to avoid hitting it.


The cat was caught by one of the cars, both cars were by now slewing under the bridge, accompanied by the cats' faces, on top of the bridge, who in a frantic and ignominious move had piled to the other side of the bridge, except for the ones whose heads were firmly stuck in the first set of railings (they were later extricated by the fire brigade). The furry totems appeared, popping through the railings again but this time on the other side, in time to see bits of cat and bursting entrails spreading across the carriageway. All this movement was unconscious; the cats were completely unaware of anything going on around them as they took in the scene from the giant bird in the sky, to the falling cat, to their heads clashing into both sets of railings, to the pureed brother or sister, for it was impossible to tell which flavour of cat it was, now smeared over a wide area. The cats with the big heads that were stuck in the first set of railings had by now snapped out of their total immersion of the moment, which ended for them with the struggle to pull their heads free and escape to the other side for the finale but they had good enough imaginations to guess what had happened. They were pissed off that they'd missed the action and that their heads were stuck in the bars, the ones with especially big heads experienced this a lot. The fire brigade knew them all by name.

'Fuck me up the arse!' Karl said with genuine shock, disbelief and pure elation. 'I got the whole thing!' Karl was the group's dude to act rationally in a crisis and was calm under pressure and by pure luck had, upon dropping from the tree on the embankment side of the fence, and seeing the cats on the bridge, put himself in the perfect position (west-side of the bridge) to film the hundreds of cats with his iPhone. He caught the whole thing on his side of the bridge, which was enough because he walked down the embankment and along the side of the road, camera still rolling, for a close up of what was left of the road-kill and then panned upwards, scanning from left to right, to the remaining heads who hadn't quite endured enough of the scene yet, still staring agog through the railings, brains absorbing the chaos. Many cats were on their way home in a state of confusion. They needed a belly rub and most would eat nothing tonight. After the near collision and backing up of traffic, the metal boxes continued on their way and then the incessant clacking of the magpies began.

Karl didn't really know what he had on his phone he was mainly filming the cat faces on the bridge but was aware of something dropping between him and the bridge that made a sickening wailing sound followed by a loud crunch when that something had hit the road. He didn't know what it actually was until he'd gone under the bridge and filmed the remains. He thought the cat had fallen from the bridge as the camera only ever went as high as the tallest totem in the railings. He had no idea it had fallen over 3000 feet. The bird had used the thermals to good effect again today as there were many nice fluffy clouds and he was dead on target. He felt good and noticed the cats that had gathered. He landed briefly on the bridge to bask in the glory of the chaos he'd created, this was a new experience, there were a lot of cats there, he'd never seen so many in one place before but then a *Dominos* delivery bike buzzed under the bridge, dodging the offal mess. The bird took flight to follow the red, white and blue coloured scooter. He could taste the BBQ sauce already. He forgot about the cats. The cats did not notice him come or go. They were awe struck.

The kids got back to Freddy's and copied the cinematic masterpiece to a desktop PC and watched the episode at least 40 times, slowing it down, rolling it backwards and forwards, all the time conjecturing the reasons why the cat had dived or been pushed from the bridge. Freddy meanwhile, bored after 5 minutes had disappeared with his laptop to watch 'African Samba Anal Fuck Orgy' on his favourite porn site. In the words of the Rolling Stones though, he couldn't get any satisfaction – his machinery just didn't function because of over use and he eventually returned to the guys frustrated and miserable, the other two knew what he'd been up to but chose to gloss over it. Although Mike had to say; 'I hope you washed your hands', 'Fuck you', Freddy returned. Freddy wasn't into the Rolling Stones, he liked Death Metal which was a furious concoction of indiscernible growling and whaling about mutilation and rape etcetera, to the backdrop of angry drumming and distorted guitars. He played it loud through his headphones as he'd been banned from playing it loud in the house, thanks to several visits from council officials as the result of multiple complaints from neighbours and passers-by. He could even hear the 'music' in his head as he walked the streets without his headphones or MP3 player. There was always noise in poor Freddy's head. Freddy would be virtually deaf by the time he died, unfortunately his death was not long coming.

'Freddy, we have to post this to YouTube and Facebook like now!' Karl said 'can we use your accounts?' Karl being Karl felt there might be a backlash of some kind and didn't want animal rights protesters burning his parents' house down or some such other shit that might materialise that he hadn't thought about yet, 'Yeah if you like,' Freddy said, who had a load of weird creepy shit on his account, that YouTube warned him about regularly, making him remove stuff all the time but he had a lot of followers. The followers multiplied a thousand times in a few short days, as the cat video went viral. Freddy was chuffed and stuck up a new profile picture of himself with his pet cat named Carrot – the cat was ginger so Freddy named him Carrot – Freddy was only 11 at the time. He really didn't give a damn about Carrot but Carrot would find the love and attention he deserved from someone else soon enough.

Freddy had 152,000 new followers on his Facebook page, he spent 3 solid days clicking accept, he loved it, becoming a celebrity overnight, although Facebook and YouTube removed the video within a couple of days as it was in bad taste and got a lot of complaints. He was on his last warning with YouTube. The sickos and morbid viewers were redirected to death-row.uk, its only content being the now famous video of cat remains smeared across a dual carriageway with the on looking and very bewildered faces of hundreds of cats heads stuck through the balustrade of a bridge that had a seagull perched on the hand rail above the bemused faces, the bird was staring directly into the camera before it flew away. It was a surreal sight and death-row.uk became very popular for a while.

# CHAPTER 16

'Oi, Franklin; have you seen that video of the cat pasted across King Offa Way?', 'no', 'aren't you and Napoleon supposed to be chasing down this cat killer?', 'yes', 'and you haven't seen the viral video that's being watched world wide of a cat being dropped from a bridge, the very same bridge that all the other dead cats have been found under in our very own Bexhill-on-sea?', 'no'.


'OI, NAPOLEAN!', 'What? Don't call me that!', 'I just asked you're girlfriend if she'd seen the video of the cat being murdered on King Offa Way', 'What? And she's not my girlfriend!', 'yeah, you know the one that's gone viral online that everyone's watching? It's making Bexhill famous all around the world', 'What?', 'Fuckwits', said Detective Sergeant Dickard at the top of his voice, upon entering the big office space with low-walled partitioned cubicles. Everyone in the room laughed aloud except for Napoleon and Franklin. Another term of endearment for Napoleon was Mofo (Mother Fucker) because he's Christian name was Maurice. The bad cops looked at each other from across, the full CID office, and after waiting an appropriate amount of time, upon the laughter subsiding and normal office background chit chat resuming, they casually strolled out of the bustling office, allowing a 5 minute gap between each departure so as not to raise suspicion among the smug elite that they were going off to find the video, the smug elite gave a conspiratorial nudge and wink to each other as each of the 'special' detectives left the room, to meet in their 'quiet place' which was a currently disused office or 'quiet zone' as the two new recruits to CID now referred to it, to search for the video on Franklin's phone, which they didn't believe existed, they just assumed it was the usual piss ripping they were on the end of on a daily basis. But they found it in seconds; before Franklin had even managed to finish typing 'cat Bexhill' the thumbnail appeared, they looked at each other and then at the video, slack jawed. Thousands around the world had already seen the video and undoubtedly many of those would have been from Bexhill which definitely included some, if not all, of their smirking colleagues.

'We need a techie to find out who posted the video' Franklin said, 'Freddy Miescher', 'What?', 'Freddy Miescher; it says under the video, I dunno, is that a picture of him underneath?', 'Oh yeah' Franklin did a couple of tiny coughs as if they would cover her humiliation but Wilkin hadn't noticed, he just wanted to be helpful, Franklin would never have to feel humiliated in front of Wilkin but she didn't know that yet. Franklin composed herself 'He looks like a kid and he's holding a bloody cat in his arms, the cocky bastard!' 'Yeah,' They tapped on Freddy's little face which gave them a bigger Freddy and some other information about the wayward teenager, Freddy wasn't concerned about his privacy and liked all the attention he could get and it saved the two police officers going to the techies for even further embarrassment. Franklin wanted to avoid the involvement of her snide colleagues at all costs and more importantly, get the bust all to herself; and Wilkin of course, so she gave her own little tech genius some time alone with her phone to see if he could find some more details about Freddy, gathering as much information on the QT, avoiding official channels, just for now. She left the quiet zone to get Wilkin a latte and a Mars bar from the vending machines outside CID, she knew what he liked.

'How's it going Maurice?' she put the coffee and Mars bar on the table Wilkin was sat at, her phone was now on the table and he was holding his own phone 'Well I thought I'd see if he was on Facebook and he was. It's the same profile pic as YouTube so it's definitely him, there's nothing about where he lives so I just sent a friend request, you never know', 'Good thinking', she meant it, she felt pride welling up for her friend, she tried to stop it but it just kept welling. She knew she would have come up with the same solution eventually. It was those idiots in CID unsettling her. Wilkin's phone vibrated. Coincidentally Freddy was at that very moment stooped bleary eyed over his laptop robotically clicking: accept, accept, accept…. to friend requests. 'Ha, I don't believe it, his accepted already, lol', Maurice straightened up and tapped on the 'About' tab and couldn't believe his luck, he looked at Franklin with a self-satisfaction and anticipated another reward from her, maybe the glint of pride he thought he'd noticed in her eyes earlier, 'He has his address and phone number on here, he's got some front!', he looked up and saw what he had hoped for, there was that faintest flash of pride again in those limpid blue eyes, which were so frequently the last things he would see in his imagination each time he went to

77

bed for his soft, fluffy sleeps. He felt like a spoiled puppy that had just been made a fuss of for the first time by its owner for begging at the back door to go outside for a poo instead of doing it on the carpet. He looked at the floor to hide his elation and fumbled at the Mars bar wrapper. He was blushing and very, very happy.

# CHAPTER 17

The sun rose into a clear, empty sky; aside from a few vapour trails left hanging in the air by jets that were returning holiday makers home after the summer breaks or taking others away. The boys had agreed to meet at the bus stop outside the Sackville Road Methodist Church at eleven o'clock to ride into Hastings for a mooch around, something they hadn't done for months, as they were spending more and more time doing their own things, Freddy was locked into his *PlayStation* and porn while Mike was basically shagging everything he could get his hands on, which was an impressive amount; chlamydia was as popular as snapchat and Facebook at the boys' school. While Karl mainly contemplated things like dead cats at this moment in time, he wasn't morbid, far from it, merely entrepreneurial.

They had a great time in Hastings, it was a wonderfully busy and sunny day and they spent the time reminiscing over days gone by, they were only young but had known each other for what had seemed, to them a very long time, sharing memories of detentions and dropping their pens under the desk to look at Teresa Parkin's vagina, which they paid her a pound ago for, they never saw much but it was a popular thing to do at the time and Teresa made a bundle.

The three sat outside *Caffè Nero* in the centre of town, soaking up the rays, with their Caramel Frappe Latte (Freddy), Frappe Milkshake (Karl) and Fruit Booster (Mike); simply relaxing, happy in each other's company, watching the locals of Hastings go about their business. Hastings is a famous town renowned around Europe for its history, it is always fit to bursting with coach loads of European students drawn to it for the historical significance of the *Battle of Hastings;* when William invaded England, although by in large, schools in the UK seemed too embarrassed to teach the country's great history; good or bad, they preferred the bad, teaching a myopic, fragmented view of the country but naturally extolled the virtues of Nelson Mandela or Ghandi. Hastings was also the famed home of television, where the local *J D Wetherspoon's* pub was named after the inventor of the world's most useful invention: John Logie Baird, who was actually Scottish but died in Bexhill, as so many people do. Mike was drooling over a 15 year old single mum pushing her black and white babies in an expensive dual pram with her left hand on the handle, mobile squeezed between her left shoulder and ear while the right hand fed a fag intermittently in to the swearing mouth, she was a big girl and wore Primark's finest, the entire ensemble was at least 2 sizes too small for her which squeezed the flab into some funny shapes, which Mike adored, 'I'd love to fuck a mum', he said, Karl just looked into the sky with a glob of whipped cream on his top lip and sighed. They really did have very little in common.

The home of television also defied the laws of natural selection, as the boys were witnessing and laughing at hysterically, for they were actually snobs, 'There's your mum Freddy', Karl said pointing at a fat woman with a walking stick and upper arms the size of giant hams that quivered at every wide arcing swing of her stumpy, retarded left leg, 'fuck you', Freddy responded with a giggle; there was nothing natural about this selection. Hastings is one of the most deprived wards in England and the locals continued about their business, to the boys' amusements, spending their benefits on cigarettes, alcohol and Frappuccino. Hastings was a veritable Petri dish, becoming a centre for culture with more and more galleries popping up in the Old Town and an ever increasing gay population too which was usually a sign of a town's regeneration, according to the news. £2:60 for a Frappuccino; where every shop was selling coffee or a haircut and they were always full up, the recession was biting hard in this town but people still needed the fundamentals.

After the excursion to the 'other side' the three teens returned to the more civilised surrounds of Bexhill-on-sea, which was considered more upmarket than its Hastings neighbour. They got off the bus early because they were hungry and all fancied a *Kentucky Fried Chicken,* which was located in Bexhill's retail park. They stood in the queue behind a father and his beautiful five year old daughter who dropped the toy she was playing with on to the floor. Her beshellsuited father said, 'For fuck's sake I just bought that fucking thing!', he had only just bought the fucking thing, from *Pound Land* 50 yards away, after he'd been in *Tescos* for his fags, before coming to *Kentucky Fried Chicken* to buy a bargain bucket for the family's dinner. They couldn't afford fresh food to cook as they were classed as poor and the two lots of child benefit along with the housing and sickness (he had a bad back) benefits that they had to manage on would not stretch to fresh fruit and veg so they relied on takeaways, they especially loved *Dominos*, but only the 2 for 1 deals on a Tuesday, '18.99 for glorified fucking cheese on toast', the mother would say 'not fucking likely!' they weren't fucking stupid. The girl would have a glittering future. She giggled at the man's tirade about the toy. The boys all looked at each other and said, 'fish and chips', they forgot their hunger because it had been such a great day and decided to walk the long distance along the seafront to the other side of Bexhill where they feasted from their favourite chip shop.

The sun was beginning to set over Bexhill. It was late August, the school holidays were coming to an end and the nights were drawing in. The iconic 1930s art deco pavilion which was the centre piece of the town cast a colossal diagonal shadow across its carpark and the adjacent sea road. The air was beginning to cool but it was a barmy evening with people still milling around with many still sitting outside the restaurants with a beer or glass of wine in hand, some were arriving for early evening meals and later, most of the restaurants would be swelled by overindulging patrons, many of whom would leave bloated and complaining that they shouldn't have had the desert.

During the hot summer days, hundreds of cars belonging to holiday makers and day trippers from London and the southeast would flock to Bexhill and its neighbouring towns. Many of the cars would end up parked diagonally facing out to sea, their noses hanging over the curb of the promenade, like the links in a giant chain, which appeared as a boundary between the long line of (recently polished) Victorian, modern and art deco style flats, B&Bs and old peoples' homes, that all stood a constant vigil over the broad, green promenade and the sea. The chain of cars snaked west to east for a mile or so to Galley Hill. As the day moved to early evening the links in the chain gradually broke formation by reversing from their spots back into the road and away, the feeling of calm and quiet slowly returned to the seafront as dusk settled in, the sun was making its journey over the town more quickly as Bexhill headed towards another autumn. The wind was picking up too.

The boys walked east along the wide promenade with their chips and battered saveloys, watching the dwindling crowds of natives and tourists after another day under a baking hot sun, winding their necks around to follow the occasional female jogger as they ran passed, to give the arse a score between 1 and 10, they never agreed. They had differing tastes; Mike liked his big and round, he even liked a bit of cellulite just so long as it was big and bouncy, he had big hands and there were plenty of big arsed joggers in Bexhill so he was happy. Karl liked a slim and pert arse, not too many of them. Nothing really worked for Freddy in the real world, he liked the ones on his screen at home, but he played along with the game anyway and was happy enough for now. There was a glorious smell of BBQs in the air from the variously sprinkled knots of people on the beach and the occasional whiff from someone sucking an e-cig. The beach would be strewn with disposable BBQs in the following dawn as the thoughtless people, when satisfied and sated, would leave their mass of empty bottles and food wrappers and carrier bags for others to deal with. It had been a glorious day though which all three friends had enjoyed. They would be back at school soon. Crap!

When the boys reached the end of the promenade, near to the *Sea Angling club* clubhouse, Freddy discarded what remained of his chips by throwing them on the ground next to one of the many bins along the seafront which, like most of the others, was overloaded with the usual takeaway containers, as well as some disposable BBQs that the less selfish had finished with and had stacked on top of or beside the dark green hexagonal bins, many of the bins had been and currently still were being ransacked by seagulls. Two seagulls appeared out of the blue and began picking up Freddy's chips before being joined by a small flock of others, most were too late. Freddy kicked one of the seagulls through the railings onto the beach as it searched for more food around his feet. The rest of the gulls quickly scattered, taking to the air or waddling off quickly as if to say 'well you ain't scaring me, I was going anyway'. Freddy didn't go out of his way to hurt things but he didn't mind hurting them, especially when they pissed him off and the seagulls' arrogance pissed him off. He felt that he deserved respect and although he'd chucked the chips away, he begrudged them taking the scraps and then hanging around him. He had a very short fuse which seemed to be becoming entirely non-existent, his body bristled with electricity which made him nervous and impatient. He could switch from happy to sad or angry in the blink of an eye.

The other two boys were flabbergasted by the violence and lack of emotion and watched the seagull, miraculously unhurt, roll back onto its feet on the beach, shake its head and body then fly off. 'What the fuck is wrong with you?' asked Mike, 'are you at, like the pre psycho stage... I mean, when are you gonna start stalking young virgins and disembowelling them? What the fuck is wrong with you? You Fucking DICK!', Mike's voice grew louder and louder and by the end of his invective he was shouting himself hoarse at Freddy, he liked animals and if the gull had been injured, would probably have punched Freddy in the face, he teetered on the precipice of whether to hit him or not, decided not but it was close. There was no love for Freddy anymore, he'd definitely been changing over the last year or so, that had been forgotten today but the three friends had stuck together almost through habit, Mike had suddenly overlooked how cordial the day had been, this violent outburst seemed to flick a switch inside him too. His tolerance for Freddy had worn out.

Freddy was becoming more remote and unpredictable. From an early age, with two very busy (high flying) career parents, Freddy was frequently left with a series of different baby sitters or au pairs. He was often left alone with only his computers and other devices for company that would pop up unsolicited sexual content (nowadays very solicited), which may have corrupted his young brain, there seemed to be a gradual loss of control leading him to seek more and more sexual and sordid material. When mum and dad were home they would give him £50 to go play with his friends. Mike and Karl were beneficiaries of Freddy's loving parents' generosity, as Freddy would spend the money on sweets and other rubbish to keep the three occupied and out of harm's way. Freddy was different back then, now he was changing, becoming less engaged and more withdrawn, darker even. He had good days but they were becoming less and less, this had been one of the rarer good days, until now. The three were slowly but definitely beginning to head in different directions. They were still, nonetheless connected for now, by a thread. The new cat phenomenon had pulled them back together from their diverging paths, or at least was still currently holding them together, however temporarily, but the strain on their relationship was telling. Freddy felt the cracks turning into chasms beneath his feet not just between his friends but with everyone. He felt alone and misunderstood. Porn brain can do this to people, as can so many other things. Freddy wanted to escape, the urge was painful because he didn't know what he wanted to escape from but the desire to runaway was becoming compulsive and this was leading him to make rash, stupid decisions, seeing the world in a distorted way. He wanted to escape but where to? He had many wants and desires but nothing fulfilled him, which led him to this point, he had zero motivation to do anything anymore not even run away, it was like a state of perpetual procrastination. Poor Freddy could not think for himself and was now feeling frustrated and angry at being judged for kicking the seagull. He looked at Karl for support.

Karl was shaking his head at the incident or rather at Freddy in disapproval but overcame it quickly to discuss the cat situation. He felt there was fame and money to be made but wasn't sure how to maximise the opportunities from their chance encounter with the cat suicide. Was it a sacrifice by the other cats or had the unfortunate cat committed a cat crime and was being punished for it by the others? He had no idea but wanted to get to the bottom of it, maybe get some more footage but today, two days after he had single handedly captured the footage, YouTube et al were pulling the gratuitous recording and death-row.uk wasn't monetised. Freddy was the computer expert and would be more than useful in this undertaking and so needed keeping on side. 'Guys, guys, the bird's okay, no harm done… Let's chillax and get back to what we filmed', 'What about it?', Mike asked, 'it's gone viral now, the whole world has seen it, people are hanging around the bridge all the time hoping it'll happen again. What are the chances of us being in the right place when it happens again? And if it happens again, at the bridge, we'll be pushing our way through the crowds that are trying to film it with their own cameras'. Karl was disconsolate because Mike was talking sense for once, and besides which, the video could and had been copied over and over, it was being shown everywhere, it's not like they could copyright it, they had lost control as soon as it had gone onto the internet, not that they ever had control of anything in the first place, it was just dumb luck that they were in the right place at the right time. The hits on death-row.uk were diminishing by the day and the footage had been shown on T.V. news channels around the globe. It was a sensation that had put Bexhill firmly on the world map but the interest was already waning.

Mike walked away, heading home across Galley Hill, still sickened by Freddy's cruelty and a bit weary of Karl's constant search for the 'next big thing'. He knew Karl thought that he was everyone's superior but Mike was losing respect for him and growing tired of his many ventures. Karl might turn out to be the next Richard Branson one day but Mike was growing bored of him and now hated Freddy, who Mike thought was a bloody weirdo not to mention a creep, he'd made up his mind to cut Freddy out of his life, the two would never talk again.

Karl watched Mike walk away and turned to say something to Freddy who was already walking off into the almost washed-out sunset, just a slither of the golden sun peeked over the majestic Beachy Head in the distance, which was the opposite direction to where Mike was heading, Karl sighed for the second time today and dropped his shoulders, propping himself on his elbows upon the silver painted railing to watch the bustling waves lap against the shore with increasing intensity, the sea was darkening and would soon appear black apart from the occasional glint of moonlight which flashed on and off behind fast moving clouds travelling up from the south, the moon was projecting a bright white, shimmering zig zagging stripe that diffused over the glistening pebbles of the beach. Karl inhaled a lungful of the crisp, cool BBQ air and thought, for the first time in his entire life, how lucky he was to live in such a place. He felt himself worry for Freddy then found himself smiling at Mike's rebellion. He hoped the battered seagull was okay too. At that moment he could swear that he heard painful screams and splashes but he strained to hear against the breeze and foaming sea lapping at the shore to hear the sounds and then they were gone. Must have been his imagination, his mind was inventing all kinds of delusions these days perhaps it was time for him to grow up. As he gazed out at the giant expanse, his eyes led by the rippling zig zag of the moonlight, he thought he could make out the black silhouette of a bird with its backside in the air, bobbing up and down.

Out to sea the front end of the huge bird emerged from the briny water and blinked salt from its eyes, as its vision cleared it could make out a be-hatted figure leaning on the railings in the distance - was it looking at him? He bobbed along with the rhythm of the high waves feeling good about the cat he'd just drowned, after menacing it for nearly 10 minutes, it was a new record for keeping the cat alive but credit to the cat it was strong and fought hard to survive, the bird stared back at the figure that appeared to stare at him. They were both enjoying life and felt at ease with the world. He shared a feeling of equanimity with his compatriot on dry land. They spent a while sharing each other's distant company, enjoying the peace and natural flow of the evening. However, there was a storm brewing and not just the one travelling up from the south, which was gathering momentum from a combination of rising warm air and moisture from the sea, but as the south wind pushed the giant clouds, they grew into one enormous tidal wave of phosphorescent grey and white, a menacing black shadow crept beneath them over the sea and would soon be stealing across the parched earth of Bexhill-on-sea. The cloud soon covered the entire region over the placid bird that was bobbing in the sea; the boy hunched over the railings and squinted as the bird disappeared into the consuming darkness. They both realised that it was time to head home. When the clouds settled over Bexhill the cooler air higher up would make them burst and Bexhill was in for thunder, wind and a good soaking from storm Suzie.

# CHAPTER 18

Behind the pavement wall of the behemoth that was the *Duper* care home, on Bexhill seafront which, contained 57 comfortably furnished rooms, lurked two, crouching figures in the shadows. PCs Franklin and Wilkin were hiding behind the care home's dense, flint wall when they had witnessed Freddy kick a seagull onto the beach. They looked at each other and smiled. These were their boys. The magical moment collapsed the shy pretence that concealed the fierceness of their passion for one another, they flung themselves at each other and snogged in a fumbling embrace, crushing the care home's azaleas in the flower bed behind the wall in the process, the pair were completely oblivious to the half dozen or so pensioners who were sat on their balconies looking down at them and wondering what they were up to, now they knew. The elderly inhabitants watched on from a high, keeping one eye on the tremendous cloud formation gathering momentum out at sea, the fumbling pair in the flower bed, were completely oblivious to the encroaching storm. The pensioners began to shiver and returned to their rooms, sliding their balcony doors closed behind them, as the outside temperature dropped palpably, the fumbling creatures in the flower bed continued the decimation of the flowers in the currently dusty grounds of the home.

By the time the amorous coppers had ruined most of the azaleas, the three kids had begun to split up and head home, when Franklin's dishevelled hair finally emerged above the care-home wall the three kids had gone, one east, one west and the other north, through 'rape alley', a long, unlit passageway which ran under the railway very near to the care home, with lots of potential dog shit to slide in, Karl used the torch app on his phone to skirt the brown menace. Franklin was annoyed by her foolishness as she'd planned to wrap this thing up as soon as possible but fortune favoured the brave and she ordered Wilkin to head off over Galley hill while she went west, to look for the boys.


Freddy wasn't aware of what went on around him at the best of times, he didn't appreciate where he lived or the things he had, unlike Karl, who he'd just walked away from. He didn't notice that there was a storm brewing and didn't feel like going home straight away, there was a lot of pent up aggression in Freddy which he needed to work off he planned to do this with a long walk along the seafront. Freddy walked from one end of the promenade to the other, from the old end with its slightly rotting wooden Victorian style shelters and benches, past the De La Warr Pavilion to the newly 'regenerated' (council lingo) west promenade which had caused much consternation and criticism from the locals. Some people don't like change especially when it costs £3.5 million, the main gripe being about the ultra-modernistic shelters that needed repairing within 6 months of their erection and which didn't keep its incumbents dry in a downpour, the narrow-minded Bexhillians were right though, the shelters were shit, the only way to keep dry was to huddle in the farthest corner and that was no guarantee of keeping dry, the landscaping was nice though. Freddy continued his trek along the long promenade, past the *Sovereign Light Café* (made famous by Keane (a pop group)) and on to the public toilets at the end of the popular area where he took the steps down onto the shingle beach before linking to another promenade made from concrete that traced the ends of wealthy gardens of homes mounted above the promenade; boasting exclusive sea views, tennis courts and swimming pools atop the mishmash of cluttered steep banks, boat sheds or dilapidated stairways, which led up to the hidden gardens. A few were lavishly finished with pristine landscaped facades. Freddy guessed some of the owners were only property rich, having bought or inherited years before they became unaffordable to the average local slave, while some of the newer owners, probably down from London or Dubai, had the cash to splash and displayed their wealth to an admiring or jealous world.

Franklin, although she didn't know it, was making ground on Freddy with her fast walk which was half skip and half jog. Freddy, meanwhile, had decided to work the muscles in his legs by ignoring the luxury of the concrete and walking on the beach instead, the storm was at least an hour away and the moon still intermittently lit up the beach, inviting him down along the line where pebbles met sand. The walk and the cooling effects of the breeze on his face did him good. As he continued his journey along the shoreline, something rolling around in the distant surf attracted his attention. He closed in on what was clearly the lank and lifeless body of a light coloured moggy, its body was being folded and unfolded by the movement of the waves, as they pushed its corpse gradually up the beach. Freddy laughed out loud and ran to pick up the lifeless body by its tail. He swung the poor, deceased creature around in circles as he walked, thinking about Karl but especially Mike who had railed against him so angrily when he had kicked the gull, he felt like he'd just got one over on the pair of them by finding the dead cat.

# Chapter 19

It had been hot for weeks and the heatwave was coming to an abrupt end. Darwin could smell the change in the weather; he liked the sunny days but enjoyed the sense of cooling dampness in the air too, so he stuck out his tongue to drink in the moisture even though he had a bowl of water in the corner of the kitchen. Darwin stood at the open door at the back of his house in Cooden, West Bexhill with his nose in the air, smelling the oncoming storm from messages sent by to him by nature through the muggy evening.

Darwin had just finished dinner and had not long returned home from a nice 'walk' with one of his owners, the one who piloted the *Shoprider Deluxe Pavement Mobility Scooter*, well it was more of a drag around than an actual walk but he didn't mind, he knew she was different to the other bipeds in the house; he always felt overwhelmingly and fiercely protective of this one. Therefore, the lack of actual walk was still loved by him and anyway, she would stop at regular intervals for him to sniff and cock either of his back legs at things. She was patient and he reciprocated that patience with understanding. He loved her. When she pottered around town he would get to ride in the basket at the front of the *Shoprider Deluxe Pavement Mobility Scooter*, which was fun over the bumpy pavements of Bexhill, he loved it. Actually, Darwin just loved, loving and being loved was his favourite thing in life but he also liked to explore on his own

95

and tonight was just right for exploring and for a little bit of 'me time' so he meandered over to the secret hole in the fence, checking that no one was at the windows to see him escape, again. He could take care of himself. He really could.


Darwin was a Jack Russell, a small but strong and sturdy breed. He was a fun, friendly and inquisitive creature and a bit more independent than most of his doggy colleagues.  He loved his owners unconditionally but he enjoyed alone time too and this seemed a particularly good night for some time to himself. Taking trouble to ensure no one from the house could see him, he took the most circuitous route around the large garden, checking with a cagey eye over both shoulders at every window and door for signs of movement, they would all be watching telly at this time of night anyway, he made his way to the overgrown (wild) part of the garden that hid the hole in the fence. He stuck his head through the hole and peered down Cooden Drive, it was a nice night for a walk he thought - he was gone.


The bird was on its way home and the change in the weather gave him a wonderful sense of freedom via the increasing winds that helped him glide, he became a passenger as the giant hand of nature effortlessly moved him around the sky, he just cupped or twisted a wing a few millimetres for height and direction. After the silent conversation with the boy in the hat had come to an end and the dark and distant figure had pushed itself away from the railing and walked off, the bird had reflected a while over the drowning cat that disappeared amidst the grey murk, dragged away by the powerful current, quickly out of sight, before the bird raised his great wings above his head for the anticipated heave of the sea that bumped him into space, propelling him high enough above the waves into the open sky, away from the increasingly turbulent ocean. Just like Freddy, he was in no mood to go home, he was restless too, and so took the long way home aiming west, as far as Pevensey Bay or Eastbourne, he wasn't sure how far to go yet, he'd just wing it for now. Meanwhile as the bird flew, the cat he'd just killed was being dragged by the powerful current at over 10 knots west to meet Freddy on the beach in Cooden.

# CHAPTER 20

Freddy was enjoying his evening promenade, the night felt mild to him after all the hot days, the breeze on his face was building and the moisture in the air was refreshing. He walked slowly along the pebbles until the muscles in his legs became weary from the stones escaping his weight; he headed back up the beach to the friendlier concrete surface that traced a line at the ends of the gardens to the lavish homes. He felt happy and began swinging the unimportant object by its tail again, in small rhythmical circles, oblivious to the shocked expressions on the faces of the infrequent passers-by. When the passers-by realised what was in the youth's hand, they did nothing except for a couple of calls made to the police but the calls were too late, as Freddy was already on a blissful trip to an ignominious end. The people who witnessed the swinging cat incident could not tell if the cat was dead or alive but did not want to interfere. The police responded to the calls but the officers sent would arrive too late to claim any glory for the cat murderer's apprehension.

Freddy turned up one of the concrete ramps that ran between the lovely houses, to avoid the shingle that the concrete walkway would soon give way to again, he headed up to small, tangled, quiet streets, moving away from the town centre. Freddy was at peace with himself by now, the cat was swinging in small arcs by his side as he meandered in the direction of home and took in the crisp, fresh air.

Franklin caught sight of the felon as he turned the corner onto a concrete ramp that she knew led to a maze of small streets, she slowed her pace to track her prey, there was the occasional civilian to consider, she needed to be mindful not to put the public in danger, after all she had no idea how dangerous the offender could be but she didn't want to lose him in the entanglement of streets above. What was that swinging by his side? 'Oh my god', she whispered to herself. He had a fresh kill and he was brazenly parading it in front of the public. How did he do it so quickly? The poor cat must have crossed his path within the 15 minutes she had lost sight of him. Was it 15 minutes? She wasn't sure. The sudden ardour between her and Wilkin had taken her by surprise, she hadn't seen him as anything but a colleague until now, his zeal for her had sparked something and her reaction was spontaneous, she wanted to be wanted, it didn't matter by whom. The cat probably went up for a friendly pat and the rotten bastard had killed it. Was it dead? She couldn't tell but she couldn't put the public in danger. She was angry at her stupidity at losing Freddy and reproved herself but the poor cat was second to public safety. She felt responsible for the cat's demise. Instinct and hours of training kicked in. Her brain was scrabbling through hundreds of procedures. She couldn't think of one for this situation. She covered her Taser with her right hand for reassurance and fumbled with her left hand for the walkie talkie on her right shoulder to call for backup from Wilkin.

Freddy thought he heard a 'kurcch' sound and looked over his shoulder. As he turned to look at where the noise had emanated, he heard a rustling that sounded like something was moving in the bushes near the bottom of the ramp. He stood for a second or two with the cat dangling by his side, staring down the ramp. He shrugged and walked on, probably just a fox or something.

Franklin stepped up her pace as Freddy disappeared from view. He was at the top of the ramp as she arrived at the bottom of it. When he turned left at the end, the static 'kurcch' sound of the walkie talkie seemed to scream into the silence of the night when Franklin depressed the talk button, making her cringe and instinctively dive over a low wire fence to her left as the boy's head turned over his right shoulder to see what the noise was. She sprang like an Olympic high jumper over the fence, performing a Fosbury flop into a thick batch of stinging nettles, making loud rustling sounds on landing. As she lay on her back in the thicket she craned her neck around, keeping as still as possible, to see the figure of the boy silhouetted by the street lights above, he stood staring down the ramp, the dead body hanging by his side. She was scared and realised she was still gripping the walkie talkie tightly in her left hand with the transmit button pushed down. After a few seconds the boy shrugged and walked on.

Adrenaline was surging through Franklin's body. She rolled onto her front and crawled to the fence, not noticing the nettles on her hands and face, she made sure that the coast was clear and climbed back over the wire fence onto the concrete ramp and sprinted to its top to see which way Freddy had gone. When she was sure that the boy was out of hearing range she whispered into the mic, 'Maurice? Maurice?.. Where are you Maurice? I've got the bastard!'

# CHAPTER 21

Wilkin's walkie talkie burped into life but then went silent, although he thought he could hear the faint crackling of bushes emit from its speaker, he paused to listen. Figuring it must be static, he continued along the long, flat coastal walk to Hastings which provided a picturesque route for amblers and cyclists. The long dark path was held together and protected from the elements by a wall of boulder sized rocks and wire. He'd caught sight of Mike, the tall gangly one dressed in an all-white tracksuit, and was hoping the others would be around too but didn't want to alert Franklin just yet, in case they weren't. He didn't want to look like a fool to her. Although he loved her, he'd always loved her really, from the very first day that they had met at training school, but there was, he felt, a bit of a competitive edge to the relationship and although he knew she was the stronger one, he still didn't want to let himself down or appear weak in her eyes. So he followed Mike along the seafront, keeping close to the tall wire fence that protected the public from the railway, which ran alongside the path for several miles. The bottom of the long fence acted like a giant fishing net catching every piece of detritus from litter bugs on land and at sea, but mainly land. The fence held onto a patchwork of: crisp packets, polystyrene fast food boxes and wrappers, pages from newspapers and magazines, plastic bags, empty poo bags and full poo bags tied to its wire mesh, as well as infinite other discarded junk.

Then Maurice heard her, a low and nervous voice calling his name. He froze with his hand pulling the walkie talkie closer to his ear. A chill ran the length of his spine and adrenalin began to surge through his system, his muscles pumped hard as he ran towards West Bexhill, the location she'd whispered into the mic. 'I'm coming, darling! Stay where you are!... Do not approach him alone! Do you hear me, Roz.. Do.. you.. hear.. me?' he puffed into the mic. It was at least 3 miles and Maurice couldn't be considered fit by any stretch of the imagination but he set off like a scalded cat, for at least the first hundred yards, gripped by panic, fighting the stich in his side which appeared surprisingly quickly. He walked with alacrity after the first half a mile taking in deep swigs of air but still really concerned about Franklin. He ran again and began to feel light headed and remembered that he'd missed breakfast because she'd called him at six in the morning, on their day off, dragging him to the park opposite Freddy's home from where they had tailed the perp, they got the term 'perp' from American T.V. shows and used it all the time, first as a joke but now all the time. They used; vics (victims) and unsub (unknown subject) among other slang terms, it made them feel like real crime fighters, and Americans. They only shared the language with each other which made the bond feel stronger to Maurice, one of their little secrets that they didn't share with the rest of the world. The rest of the world would laugh if they knew, especially the tossers in CID. Maurice didn't care now. He just wanted to save the woman he loved. He'd missed lunch and dinner too, come to think of it but at least he'd had a few coffees in Hastings which had given him a slightly spaced out feeling.

One and half miles on, Maurice realised his sporadic running was no longer in a straight line, he was weaving from side to side as he became fainter and fainter from the lack of food or fluids during the long hot day. The two didn't think to pack anything to eat or drink before they had decided to sneak around the local area following Freddy and his friends, who had converged at a bus stop and then spent the day milling aimlessly around Hastings. While the boys were in *Neros* the two detectives were opposite in *Costa,* they could have sat in *Jempsons* but Roz preferred *Costa*. The town was awash with coffee shops and cafes. Hastings was a slightly rough around the edges, café society but he had enjoyed his day with Franklin immensely and while she stared fixedly at the boys he would steal furtive looks at her. He remembered a doughnut and a Belgian bun – why did he feel so tired and hungry? After a long day of coffee and subterfuge around Hastings and Bexhill, the two American cops finally hit pay dirt, hours of surveillance in stifling temperatures culminated in; while crouching behind the wall of an old peoples' home, the witnessing of Freddy's vindictive act against the seagull on the promenade. The couple were overcome by the overwhelming chemical reaction released upon solving the crime of the century, or was it just sheer relief? He liked the word couple. After groping in the flower bed of the old peoples' home they lost the gang of cat killers that they had tracked so successfully all day long, without the bastards even suspecting that they were being tailed. Damn! How could they have been so stupid? He didn't regret it though at least it was out now, their feelings for each other, the cat was out the bag and it wasn't going back in, not if he had anything to do with it.

Maurice woke from his dream to find himself staring at the sky that contained big dark clouds that were moving in a fast northerly direction above him, light rain brushed his face, bringing him round, oh so gently but the movement of the clouds made him feel dizzy and sick. Apart from Franklin and the lovely day they had shared he had been dreaming about eating oranges, lots and lots of lovely, sweet and succulent oranges, he couldn't get enough of them; then he suddenly snapped back to reality, confused and wondering how long he'd been out for, he shouted 'Roz!' the rain felt good around his face and lips. He struggled to his feet, feeling light headed again, he stood up too quickly but then started to run again (it felt like running), only two miles to go? He squeezed the transmit button on the walkie talkie and panted into the mic 'I'm coming Roz! Where, are you now?', 'kurcch'.

# CHAPTER 22

'Kurcch' God damn it! Roz had forgotten to turn the volume down on her walkie talkie, she dived head first over a low wall to someone's front garden and lay motionless on her back on a concrete hedgehog, not daring to move an inch, except to turn off the walkie talkie. Then after a few seconds she rolled onto her front and crawled army style to the wall, slowly raising herself up to her knees, she peeked through a large lavender bush which overflowed the garden onto the pavement. She saw Freddy walking away, picking up the pace. She clambered over the low wall to continue the pursuit feeling more confident but worried that she may have been given away by Maurice and the walkie talkie. Her back hurt from the concrete hedgehog and her face and hands began to itch like as the pain killing effects of adrenalin slowly wore off, she was becoming more confident at stalking her prey now, her hand was still pressed firmly on the Taser.

What the fuck is that fucking Kurch noise? He'd heard it twice now. Freddy turned around to look into the shadows behind him. There was nothing there except for a massive lavender bush swaying in Suzie's accumulating winds; her skirts would be billowing tonight, displacing so many plants and objects that were in her path of destruction, the lavender would survive the night though. He headed on towards home, starting to feel his more normal, anxious self. He'd forgotten the cat in his hand

and increased his speed. He just wanted to get home now. The calm, assured leisurely gait became a disjointed hustle with furtive, flitting looks over each shoulder. Was it his imagination? Too scared to take a proper look, fear was beginning to grip Freddy. He was sure he was being followed. His mind began to race and he thought of that foreign student nearly kicked to death in broad daylight along the seafront. A black, fugacious shadow was in his peripheral vision every time he dared to take a look behind, he ran, nearly tripping over a stray Jack Russell that appeared to be eating a dog turd on the corner of Cooden Drive. The shadow ran too.

The Taser felt good pressed between her hip and her itchy hand, it gave her an unnatural confidence and the target was in her sights. And the target ran. So she ran too. No more hiding in the shadows. She wasn't scared any more. Franklin had already decided to Taser the evil bastard and claim self-defence. Bloody hell he was fast. Franklin was fitter than Wilkin but she only had little legs and the felon was easing away. She pirouetted around a stray dog and focussed on the diminishing figure ahead.

Freddy fearing for his life began to sprint onto Cooden Drive, which was a big road and well lit, hoping that the shadow would give up the chase. As he turned into Cooden Drive the cat slapped his right thigh which snapped Freddy back to reality. He had a dead cat in his hand. What the fuck? Just a few yards ahead he saw a skip on the front lawn of a house that was being renovated and decided to ditch the cat there. He was looking over his shoulder constantly by now and couldn't see any sign of the black figure or hear any footsteps which surprised him because he was no Usain Bolt. His imagination had been running riot lately; maybe he'd just imagined the psycho killer hot on his heels. The exercise had cleared his head a bit and he had made a mental note to himself to cut down on the horror films and go easier on the porn. He needed to get out more. He chuckled nervously to himself as he stepped onto the driveway of the house to deposit the cat into the skip. He was knackered and was sweating heavily but the misty moisture and wind from Suzie was cooling him down, enabling him to recover his senses. Freddy crossed the threshold of the expensive property, but while lifting the cat over the lip of the dented, rusty, yellow skip, security lights snapped on; 500 watts of bright, white halogen light lit him up like an Oscar ceremony. 'FREEZE! Put the cat down and move away from the skip.. NOW!' a female voice shouted from behind him, the 'now' was a high pitched shrill bordering on a shaking, maniacal scream.

Like a rabbit caught in the headlights Freddy did freeze but then panicked and ran away again with the cat still in tow. After a couple of minutes of frenzied, directionless running he realised he still had the cat and chucked it over a fence into a kids' playground. The cat finished up in a sandpit after bouncing off of a wooden motorbike, mounted on a giant spring which the kids could rock around on in every direction. The cat was vital evidence and its picture would become famous around the world as the cat that caught the killer. Its name was Bahji. The owners of Bahji wanted to remain anonymous but were extremely upset and angry and wanted justice, they would not get it. The public would be disappointed that behind the cat phenomenon was just another twisted human, which is so often the case with mysteries. Most knew but wanted to believe in ritualistic cat on cat sacrifice. It did look that way on YouTube but the human must have been crouching behind the cats on the bridge somewhere while his friends captured it on film. How did he get so many cats onto the bridge? So many questions would be left unanswered. Forensics discovered that the cat had been drowned in the sea so the bastard had caught the cat, carried it to the sea and held the poor thing under the water, the evil bastard!

# Chapter 23

The bird was enjoying its journey home. It had flown as far as Eastbourne, not intending to but caught up in the moment, he had travelled the five miles in as many minutes. He was now on his way back home to Bexhill tracing the route along the seafront and the great stretch of road that was Cooden Drive, when he noticed something, a little something that took his fancy; Darwin's wagging tail. He knew the difference between a cat and a dog. A dog would never try to jump on to a roof of a bungalow but this animal was roughly the same size as the cats he'd been used to catching so, what the hell, he prepared to dive.

Darwin completely oblivious of being watched from the sky had been walking towards town, once he'd peed over a smell he'd found on a lamp post he was on his way again. He'd indulged in bit of un-bagged coprophagia (eating shit) which is something his owners would shout red faced at him to stop doing, before he'd been distracted by the delightful smell on the lamp post. Darwin liked being out on his own and had no idea that a winged demon was dropping from the sky above to grab his very happy head and take him for a flying lesson.

Early in the outing Darwin had bumped into Butch, a friend and fellow vagabond, Butch was a young, heavyset Bulldog and they enjoyed each other's company, so Butch accompanied Darwin for a while on this windy evening, on the opposite side of the street. Butch was badly designed and constantly licked his lips and sneezed which got on his nerves, he'd occasionally lose sight of his little mate who was sniffing the lamp posts on the opposite side of the road, and didn't share Darwin's love of poo eating. They didn't have much in common and were unlikely friends but they liked to share this big street together when their outings coincided. The air was wet and Darwin's head was slick with rain. He wasn't overly keen on rain, he liked a bit of it now and then but not the heavy stuff that made it hard to see, the heavy stuff was on its way, he could sense it, he'd nibbled some shit and peed up a few walls and lamp posts so it hadn't been a bad night, he was thinking of heading home, when something grabbed his head and pulled him into the air.

The bird had switched to autopilot once more and was compensating for the wet, slightly turbulent conditions at ground level, as it skirted a foot and half above the pavement. It had to judge well, grabbing the dog half way between the evenly spaced lamp posts its wide wing span could easily catch the lamp posts on the edge of the pavement as it flew inches away from the garden walls on the other side of the pavement. It clasped the greasy little head but before the dog's feet had left the ground the bird was hit by a sudden sense of Déjà vu. How can this thing be so heavy? Jack Russells are densely packed bundles of muscle and although Darwin was not much heavier than an average cat he was a strong physical presence, the weight and movement under the bird, combined with a different architecture between cat and dog skulls meant that the bird could not hold on to the little head and manoeuvre at the same time. It let go. Unfortunately for the bird Darwin was well practiced at catching things, sticks in particular and when released Darwin had made a spectacular Kung-Fu like flip and lunge in mid-air at the bird's left leg which looked remarkably like a stick to Darwin who held on tight. This was a strong bird but it could not lift the Jack Russell and the weight that had shifted over to its left side pulled it into one of the big front gardens of Cooden Drive where it ditched.

Butch was cocking his leg up a lamp post and sneezing at the time that the bird took his friend away, as his vision cleared from the last batch of sneezes, he couldn't believe what he saw and set off immediately across the broad road to chase the apparition that was of a bird and his friend. But Butch was heavyset and slow, he tried barking but sneezed instead, he had a sensitive, squashed nose and the fine misty rain was playing havoc with his vision and other senses tonight. He was almost hit by a speeding police car that was racing down Cooden Drive with its red and blues ablaze.

The bird was up-side down rectrices over beak again with its feet dangling just under (or above depending on one's point of view) its beak, its body shaped like a big letter C, it blinked several times and found itself staring into the face of the dog which was curiously the same way up as the bird with its tongue hanging out onto the wet grass in front of its left eye, its tail wagging like a windscreen wiper between its back paws which were slowly dropping nearer to the ground, either side of its head. Darwin had a new friend. Enthusiasm not fear had brought them clattering to the ground. Riding in the basket on the front of his mum's *Shoprider Deluxe Pavement Mobility Scooter* over the lumps and bumps of the pavements of Bexhill was nothing compared to this. The new friend didn't hang around though, flipping the right way up, it ran a short distance before launching itself back into the sky, Darwin just missed out on catching the stick that the bird held so tantalisingly near to him, beneath its giant body. Darwin had to settle for watching the white phantom, with longing eyes, as it receded into the ever turbulent, wet and darkening sky, with the sticks trailing below, Darwin liked this new game. Butch arrived just in time to see the bird disappear into the gloom, worn out he plonked himself down next to the animated Darwin and sneezed. Darwin waited until his new friend had completely vanished and was sure that there would be no repeat performance, before standing up, shaking himself off and walking away with a smile on his face and a wagging tail, in truth the tail had not stopped wagging since he had headed out for the 'me time', he was a very happy dog, his tail even wagged in his sleep sometimes. He said goodbye to Butch and headed home. Upon sneaking back indoors unnoticed, he parked himself on the rug in the centre of the living room, soaked his family who were all watching telly with one last whole body shake, closed his eyes and dreamed of flying and of his new friend with the pink stick. Unfortunately the *Shoprider Deluxe Pavement Mobility Scooter* would never be the same again, although it did have one ace left up its sleeve.

# CHAPTER 24

Sweat, rain and tears flowed down Freddy's cheeks as he sprinted for home. The 'Freeze' part of the woman's statement was beginning to sink in as he realised that he was being chased by the police and that running away with a dead cat in hand, when the current popular topic of conversation in the media and around town was that of the mysterious appearances of cat corpses littering Bexhill, may appear suspicious. In fact, the more he came to think of it, as he ran his body to exhaustion, walking along the seafront brazenly swinging the cat around in full public view, probably didn't do him any favours either. His brain worked frantically on various permutations and ways out of the mess. He couldn't find a way out but he was innocent. He found the cat, okay, swinging it around wasn't the most appropriate of actions to take but he hadn't actually done anything wrong, not as in actually killing it anyway.

Freddy was leaving the small police woman in his wake. He definitely had the legs on her and was becoming confident that he could escape. All of a sudden sirens sounded ahead, he could see blue lights through the drizzle instinctively he swerved to his right into St Augustine's Close, a dead end. He stopped and bent over with hands on knees clutching for breath, heaving his belly in and out, in the shadow of a white ash tree, the police car sped past the opening to St Augustine's. With mild relief he began to relax a little, dropped his shoulders and poked his head around the corner, upon which he saw the relentless pursuit of the little police woman, sprinting up Cooden Drive eyes fixed on his location, she'd seen him. The police car on passing its colleague hit the brakes, the harsh red brake lights cut through the dim wet air, silhouetting PC Franklin who cut through the red and blue flashing mist with high knees and pumping arms.

Freddy ran again hoping to find a way out or somewhere to hide but there was no way out and nowhere to hide. He ran across a kind of village green, made slippery by the rain, towards a church, while constantly on the lookout for other roads or exits to run down. 'STOP!' the voice came again, she was like some fricking super woman. How the hell was he going to shake her? He reached the church as the police car entered St Augustine's, its headlights throwing Freddy and Franklin's shadows up against the wall of the church in sharp relief.  He rounded the front of the church hoping for a twitten to escape down but there was just a wall and some big commercial bins. It fleeted through his mind to jump in a bin but he'd already by this time given up all hope of eluding the force of nature that was chasing him, cornered and defeated, he turned with his back to the bins and his hands in the air, wanting it all over with, exhausted and trembling with fear.

He watched, in slow motion it seemed, as wonder woman entered the small courtyard whereupon catching sight of him, dropped her right hand to her hip and pulled something up to point at him, there was a flash of light. Freddy expected his rights to be read to him, not this. He woke up in hospital four hours later.

Catching up with Freddy, as he was about to drop the cat into a skip, fortuitously lit by someone's security lights, she shouted the loudest 'Freeze' she could muster but the bugger had just turned and fled again, continuing up Cooden Drive. Although she'd feared the end of the chase because she didn't know if the perp would fight for his freedom, she also wanted it over with because she was completely knackered and frustrated and now he was disappearing into the distance again. She wanted to shoot him more than ever with the Taser but she'd fumbled the electrocuting device from its clip and dropped it on the wet ground, it skittered away from her and when she bent to pick it up it slipped out of her rain soaked and sweaty hand again and by the time she stood to take aim, he'd gone. She hoped she'd get a second chance and have the balls to do what was needed when it came to the crunch. 'Fuck and bollocks!' just what she didn't need, he was disposing of the evidence over a fence, if only she hadn't spilled the Taser she'd have nailed him with it, she watched on hopelessly, as the cat cartwheeled over the fence. Well, she'd witnessed it all anyway which should be enough, the cat could be found later, after the scum bag had been caught and the two put together, there's probably DNA evidence.

117

She sprinted on with the forlorn hope that he would trip or suffer a heart attack but he was disappearing into the ever increasing gloominess of the wet and stormy night. Blue lights? Her spirits lifted two or three notches at the sight of her colleagues as she became imbued with a sense of comfort and support but then quickly dropped a notch when she realised that they could steal the collar from her and interfere with her plan. She wanted to Taser her first victim. Just as the lights and siren cut through the gloom she saw Freddy's right shoulder drop and he was gone. Good, he'd seen the police car and he was either hiding or, she knew that road from her time on the beat there was no exit, he was trapped. He was hers for the taking. She needed this, she needed it so badly, and the need fed the grit and determination which drove her on. She hated being a woman in the police force; she knew she was thought less of by her male colleagues who resented the preferential treatment accorded to women and other groups, but mainly women, by over compensating 'equality acts' the men also believed that the fairer sex was the weaker sex. She felt that the increasing amount of women who came into to the service only to fall pregnant and claim maternity leave for a year didn't help her cause. She didn't want to be tarred with the same brush, she didn't want kids, what she really wanted was to prove that she could do the job of any man, of ten men! And she wanted whoever she was partnered with to know that she had the wherewithal to 'have their back' when a situation became serious. Most of all she wanted to be trusted and respected not ridiculed. She believed in herself and now it was her chance to prove herself to the rest.

As she ran she realised that the police car may just have been on a shout and have nothing to do with her, or Maurice may have called it in when he lost walkie talkie contact. Regardless, Freddy was out of sight now and they might just think she was a jogger and pass on by, she put her head down. The car shot by and then came to a clamorous halt. She could sense the hurried stop of the vehicle over her left shoulder by the intermitted sucking of rubber on wet tarmac from the car's anti-lock brakes. Throwing caution to the wind, she sprinted into St Augustine's, taking a risk that the fiend may be hiding around the first corner waiting to pounce, her eyes ready to dart from every dark nook to every deep cranny but within a nanosecond she saw him running across the big green, heading for the church. It looked like he was running on water the green was a shimmering black under the sodium glare of the street lights.


She felt like she was now the hunter and the hunted at the same time and the sight of Freddy, who had now disappeared again, this time behind the church, spurred her onwards. Her shadow, made by the penetrating, headlights of the police car, grew bigger and bigger upon the church wall as she reached nearer and nearer to the finale of a debilitating foot race. There was no fear or trepidation any more only an acute sense of getting the job done before the car arrived. She rounded the church and saw the figure of a shivering 14 year old boy with his hands held aloft, it looked like he was about to say something, her hand went assuredly to the weapon, it didn't fumble, it didn't slip, it unclipped and lifted the mean, yellow plastic beast that

119

contained immense, stored energy, took aim and fired, instinct. She was the hunter!

Franklin was small, Freddy was average, they were on an incline, Freddy was higher than Franklin and Franklin's Taser training taught her to fire low to avoid the face or direct contact over the heart. Therefore, the two barbs fired from the gun scored a direct hit at Freddy's testicles, passing nicely through the soft flesh of the scrotum and hooking tightly onto one ball each. 50,000 volts exploded through Freddy's testicles, he swore later that he could see God through a blinding light. He would find later that god had no sense of humour.

'Fuck!', Dave slammed hard on to the brakes to avoid a bulldog that appeared form the murk to run in front of the police car, 'Ere Dave', 'Yeah?', 'Ain't that the shrimps girlfriend?', 'Blimey, yeah I think it is. Why the hell is she running around in the dark and the rain?', 'Ain't she on the cat case?.... Stop the car now!' PCs; Dave Spencer and Si Bent were sent to search for a suspect walking around the promenade, apparently swinging a dead cat around. It seemed too much of a coincidence to Si that his diminutive colleague should be sprinting in the rain this evening in the same vicinity that the 999 calls had reported the youth with the cat to be. 'She must be on to something, turnaround and follow her' Si said, while looking over his left shoulder so as not to lose sight of her, he lost sight of her as she turned into St

Augustine's. 'She's gone into St Augustine's.. Hurry up Dave!' Dave already had the BMW's tail dancing around in a semi-doughnut and was on his way. The two didn't notice a giant seagull swooping along the ground on the opposite side of the car, skimming two feet from the pavement with a Jack Russell wagging its entire body beneath it, for they were in hot pursuit, eyes fixed upon the entrance to St Augustine's Close.

When Si and Dave had entered St Augustine's they saw two figures running in a straight line to St Augustine's church, the first figure they could barely make out, looked like a man and he'd already reached the church and disappeared around its facade, Franklin was hot on his heels but the car couldn't go across the green, instead it peeled off to the right of the tree lined green around the narrow road where visibility of Franklin, who flickered on and off through the trees, was lost by the time they had rounded the church front, where they discovered some bins, their colleague and the prone teenager, they'd missed all the action, they were gutted.

Si and Dave got out of the car and ran to Franklin who stood shaking over the body, Taser still clasped in both hands. Thick black, blood mixed with the rain and ran down the incline of the grey concrete yard, fortunately the dead weight from Freddy's head that pressed down onto to the hard ground helped stem some of the initial blood loss. Si radioed in for an ambulance

121

while crouching over Freddy, reaching for his neck to feel for a pulse in the boy's carotid artery. Dave was trying to get Franklin to talk, she was shivering, frozen, rooted to the spot, he gently attempted to pull the Taser from her grasp, she let go. 'It's okay Roz. It is Roz isn't it? Do you remember me? I'm Dave Spencer we've sort of met a couple of times but not properly, he said the words in a soothing tone, trained as he was in this sort of thing, victim support. He saw Rosalind, in this moment, as a colleague and a victim and he needed to get some kind of statement out of her. The police had been getting some bad press recently for unjustified use of Tasers, fucking liberals, Dave thought to himself. Therefore, he wanted to make sure that she got her story straight. Not just for her but for the police in general, whether it was true or not. Dave and Si had arrived at the scene almost at the same time that Franklin had, and Dave suspected that there was not enough time for the guy now lying face down on the ground, to have attacked her.

Si did all the right things for Freddy, he was actually considering changing careers and training to be a paramedic, he was tired of the routine domestics and drunks and had always had an interest in the human body, on his days off he studied from a stack of biology and medicine books he'd acquired from various used book stores and was a member of *St John ambulance*, although he didn't get to go along very often due to his shift patterns with the police. Maybe he just needed a change. Could he afford it? He didn't know but regardless of what Si's future held for him he was still a policeman and fiercely loyal and protective of his colleagues, even the ones he had doubts about. He had some huge doubts now but kept a calm perspective. He would help his colleague.

'He came at you, he was trapped, he was angry, he'd just killed a cat, you knew that physically you were no match for the angry young man, and wouldn't be able to restrain him, the only way, the last resort, was to go for the Taser', Dave said. 'How old do you reckon he is?' asked Si, upon returning to the police car, he looked into the back seat where Franklin sat soaked, looking tiny and dishevelled in the back of the big BMW. She watched as Freddy's limp, lifeless body was lifted into the back of an ambulance by the paramedics, a drip with saline and paracetamol was being held by one of the paramedics who then hooked the bag of fluid onto something when they had Freddy secured in the ambulance. Freddy was in a carry chair and sat in the ambulance facing the police car, looking like a bloody, wax work dummy, he appeared to be staring at Franklin through the illuminated darkness of St Augustine's Close but Freddy's eyes were firmly closed. Rain slapped hard against the windscreen of the car like a heavy curtain of water and Freddy disappeared as the blurry image of two yellow doors came together. He is 14, he was scared, he had his hands in the air to surrender, and he was crying, he is 14, she shot him. 'The public will be on your side, you caught the cat killer, the nasty bastard, and everyone hates him. It was self-defence Rosalind.' Dave said. She watched the blurry images of the yellow ambulance doors slamming shut to hide the bloody face of the unconscious boy and then after a couple of minutes the ambulance drove away, blue lights flashing. Dave and Si looked at each other; Franklin hadn't said a single word since the incident, they both turned to face the windscreen and then they set off for the 25 minute trip to A&E, in complete silence.

# CHAPTER 25

Luckily for Freddy the pain from 50,000 volts passing through his nuts was so exquisite that he passed out almost instantly. Unluckily for Freddy the pain was still there for a long time after he had woken up again. Luckily for Freddy he wasn't aware, at the time, of his nose and right cheek bone splintering as they greeted concrete when he fell flat on his face with arms flapping uselessly by his sides. Unluckily for Freddy his face was as swollen as his balls, which were like black and blue coconuts, small ones, by the time he woke up in a hospital bed, legs akimbo; a stocky, mono-browed, wispy moustachioed health care assistant, called Katy, dashed to get a Doctor as soon as she'd noticed Freddy's blood shot and blackened eyes, blinking through the 'invisible man mask' of bandages wrapped around his head, he blinked against the bright, sterile lights above his bed.

Franklin had been examined and was given the all clear, apart from suffering severe dehydration. She, like Wilkin, had gone all day with very little food or drink. Her demeanour suggested that she would need some form of counselling though. She had, against doctor's orders, insisted on sitting in the hallway outside of Freddy's room, she was attached to a drip which replenishing her fluids and returning her mind to the moment. She feared the extent of the harm she had caused to Freddy, hoping against hope that there was no permanent damage.

Angry welts covered her face and hands from scrabbling around in brambles and her back was developing a big, black bruise from lying on an ornamental concrete hedgehog, the pain made her shift frequently from cheek to cheek in the chair to find a comfortable place. It would be a while before she found a comfortable place. Now that the effects of shivering; caused by shock, adrenalin and dehydration were losing their effect, they were making way to itching, pain and guilt. She was gradually moving from the surreal to the real and it made her more and more uncomfortable. Si and Dave kept wary eyes on her, as she scratched her face and hands and constantly transferred her weight from one buttock to the other. She seemed to be gibbering something to herself too. Si and Dave were worried.


Wilkin was found unconscious by a member of the public walking their dog, approximately a mile away from the scene of the assault on Freddy, which is what it was. He was in a separate cubicle with a drip attached to his left arm, dreaming about oranges, great big, juicy oranges. A member of child services walked past the curtain of his cubicle heading for Freddy's room followed by a reporter from the *Bexhill/Hastings Onlooker*. Dave and Si were cowered in a cubicle while the district commander, who had been called by the hospital, stood over them she was in an incandescent rage making them relive the scene over and over again for her but they luckily hadn't seen anything, she'd already seen Franklin outside Freddy's room and bent over her, for several minutes, with her hands on her knees simply staring into Franklin's vacant eyes, saying nothing, seething with anger.

If Si and Dave were not about to break soon under this incessant barrage of questioning by the District Commander, they felt their resolve melt when the Assistant Chief Constable Malky Fry poked his head into the cubicle in search of the angry, one-sided tirade. But to Dave and Si's unlimited gratitude he was there as the hand of reason and pulled the District Commander out of the cubicle and away from the very relieved Bobbies. Fry had been called in by the higher powers to bring the situation under control, the news was spreading like a forest fire and the police were worried, the press were excited and the social workers and parents were fuming. The biggest surprise was that Franklin's meteoric career dash was only temporarily upset, within a few short years she would be working quite closely with the present incumbent of the District Commander role, who herself would move on to even bigger and better things, due in large part to this incident. The higher powers within in the police collaborated with other services but were tight lipped with the press and any other outsider. Franklin had caught the cat killer of Bexhill, after all. At least the public would be appeased on that front. And they would never know about the black and blue youth currently residing in a hospital bed just next door to A&E.

After the District Commander had been removed from the equation, Dave and Si took turns with Franklin, moving a chair beside her while she sat uncomfortably outside Freddy's room. They were whispering the format of what happened. Simply; the boy ran, dumped the cat, was cornered and launched himself, threateningly, fists clenched, shouting at her, she knew she couldn't restrain the boy, she only had one option. Things happened fast she didn't want to do it, it was a last resort. Franklin's brain filtered the information without showing any physical signs to Si or Dave that she was taking anything in. It was a story she'd already concocted for herself and rehearsed during the chase. Gradually it began to sink in and make sense again. Si finally convinced her to move to a secluded cubicle. While Dave and Malky Fry fielded the press and child services, Franklin finally slept.

Hurricane Suzie wreaked havoc that night. Freddy wasn't the only one that was left feeling sore. Bexhill had taken a pounding with flash floods, uprooted sheds and greenhouses, broken fences and the odd tree crushed car. One such car contained a man attempting to reverse into his driveway. He was killed along with a hapless rescuer. There was a lot of news to report on that night and the *Onlooker's* journalists were stretched, which gave the police some breathing space to regroup. The protective shield was raised and fierce discussions and negotiations with other services to protect the sanctity of the brother and sisterhood ensued. The two tragic deaths, plus a third that night helped cover over some cracks.

During the myriad of tests and scans that ensued, a particularly keen young doctor spotted signs of something neuro as Freddy's dilated pupils staggered around when asked to follow the doctor's finger during a routine test, it was just a hunch but he ran some extra tests, tests that Freddy had already had 12 years prior but the results were the same. Freddy had a rogue gene, his family already knew about this but they had never told Freddy. When should they have told him, what was the right age, how could they tell him? It was easier not to. Freddy's mother was not as strong as her own mum who had had to deal with it on her own, it seemed like another lifetime ago, and yet sometimes it felt like yesterday. 12 years of denial. Consequently, Freddy led an isolated existence, his mum and dad avoided him, too distracted by the 'important' things which kept the family in the luxury that they were all very much accustomed too, Freddy missed them both.

# CHAPTER 26

Mr Shepstone at number 12 was looking out of his front room window at the darkening sky and swirling shrubs and trees. He always kept up-to-date with the news and weather, the usually ebullient Simon 'Perky' Parkin on *Meridian News* was giving a 'serious' weather warning over Mr Shepstone's left shoulder. Shepstone was thinking about battening down the hatches. He was worried about his wheelie bins in particular. Just as he was thinking about his precious bins, one of the now defunct green plastic boxes that had been used for paper recycling, before the big green wheelie bins superseded it, the green wheelies could take tins *and* paper *and* other stuff (though the council still buried it in landfill), skipped and hopped down the street just missing Shepstone's car, which he had left parked in the street while he mowed the lawn earlier in the day. It had been a sunny day and he had run the lead for the mower from the garage out to the front lawn and brought out an assortment of his scrape and sweep tools. He was in and out of the garage many times that day collecting different implements for different (specific) jobs. The skipping green box minus its lid had just missed Shepstone's car but smacked into Dave Rogers' Toyota, Shepstone sniggered, for he didn't like Dave, ever since Shepstone had lent Dave his electric sheers that were returned, eventually, filthy and blunt. It was pure luck that Shepstone had had to park on the opposite side of the road, as Dave had parked his *Rav4* where Shepstone usually parked his Jag. Ha, fuck you Dave!

It had been a fine day and he'd just put all his gardening things back in the garage when Mavis called him in for his tea. All his tools and gardening paraphernalia had their place and he checked several times that the inside of the garage looked just right before he went contentedly in for his tea. In the 45 minutes it took to eat his tea and six chocolate fingers the sky had blackened and Shepstone now stood staring through the living room window at the oak tree opposite his house, the tree was bending threateningly over his prized Jag as if a giant's foot were pushing it in the direction of Shepstone's house before snapping back again as the giant gave up, moving on to harass some other innocent object like the green recycle bin it had just kicked down the street into Dave's car.

Shepstone reached a decision, 'I'm sticking the wheelie bins in the garage and bringing the car in!' he was talking to himself, Mavis wasn't interested. Opening the front door he was almost sucked off of his feet and blown back in doors, the air was damp and he hadn't put his coat on because it was to be a quick manoeuvre. Forcing his head down, he fought against the elements. After he'd hustled the three wheelie bins into the calm protection of the garage he headed for the car. The car door was wrenched from his clutches, cracking hard against its metal stop, 'Fuck!', there was no time to check for damage, he needed to get the big Jag onto the cramped driveway; he turned the engine on, the lights came on automatically against the impending darkness. He put the car into reverse, looked over his shoulder, four tonnes of oak slammed onto the roof of the Jag.

131

The Jag was a very big car and looked like it could stand its ground in most situations but all four tyres burst milliseconds after its windows exploded outwards, the roof folded like tin foil crushing Shepstone, whose head was still looking over his right shoulder; this was the position in which he died, pressed down beneath the roof with his head crammed between the door post and the side of the luxurious leather driver's seat. He would often rest his elbow proudly on the door ledge when he cruised around East Sussex in his shiny black pride and joy-mobile.

Mavis was settling down with a coffee and the rest of the chocolate fingers to watch *strictly* on the telly when an almighty blast shook the ground and made the windows wobble, the force was followed by the wailing of several car alarms, the chocolate fingers were thrown in the air but she saved the coffee and managed to put the mug down safely on the table next to her armchair. She ran to the window, drawing back the curtain to reveal the top of the oak tree scraping the tips of its leaved branches, like long finger tips scratching against the front windows of her house, the old tree was resting on her lawn, flashing amber, on and off, through what was left of its leaves, which danced freely, swirling amidst the busy wind. She knew what had happened but she couldn't quite reconcile it. Was the oak tree from over the road really now covering her front lawn? She could just about make out the front of the Jag through the wildly animated fronds of the tree that lifted up and crashed back down, lifted and crashed, like a Mexican Wave, the screech of the glass made her spine shiver and broke her from a fugue state. Their lives together hadn't been all bad, they'd had some wonderful times actually and he used to be a very funny man, her arms were moving as if they were telling the rest of her body to do something when, finally, the brain engaged and she accepted the extraordinary site; her body moved eventually with wildly quivering limbs over to the phone to call 999, she found it difficult to support her very light weight. She couldn't go outside.


Shepstone's body was pinned but he was aware that his legs were hot and his shoes were filling with a warm liquid, he hoped he hadn't pissed himself. He hadn't pissed himself, the warm liquid was blood from his left femoral artery which had been punctured by a jagged piece of oak that pierced the metal roof like a fork through cheese cake; in four or five minutes there would be no blood left for his heart to pump, he had around seven minutes left to reflect on his life, or maybe six lucid ones, before lack of oxygen removed sensible thought. His head was bashed but he was thinking clearly. He felt no pain at all but was aware of the plush leather heated seat squeezing the right side of his face into the seat belt strap. The roof had come crashing down on him as he craned his neck round to look over his shoulder to back the car into the drive; he thought about Mavis, for approximately three and half minutes, when they had first met at work and shared lunchtimes, the palpitations he had felt when he anticipated seeing her each day, he felt them now as if it was 25 years ago, he took her for granted now, 'You're a bastard Duncan, a bastard', he thought he said the words out loud but he couldn't move his mouth so maybe he hadn't, then he wondered if the Jag could be fixed and was relieved that the bins had been put in the garage, had he locked the garage? He spent a minute or so trying to remember, then suddenly realised it was the brown bin's turn to go out, garden waste, to go out on Tuesday, he'd just done the garden so the bin was nearly full up. What day was it today? The last thing Shepstone was aware of was the dull thunk of another green recycle box hitting metal; it struck the boot of his Jag, although thankfully he couldn't tell this, he assumed it was Dave's again. After one last futile pump; Shepstone's heart stopped, there was nothing left to pump, all the blood was in the foot-well of the car. Duncan Shepstone had become bored with life since retiring, where boredom sometimes leads one to seek out more challenges, his boredom and feelings of entitlement to do nothing, fuelled procrastination and anger and bitterness, he made up hypothetical arguments with neighbours who he had never met. Shepstone's resentment of life had all focused on to one person, Mavis. She didn't mourn him long.


Matt was 22 and an idealist, he was a good lad with a strong moral code and his own sense of what was right. The young, handsome fireman had joined the brigade to do something good with his life and he was fastidious in his training and a good and trusted member of the team, everyone liked him. Now he stood, at 6 feet tall, dwarfed by the roots of the up-turned tree, thinking about his training and all the procedures that he and his colleagues were supposed to strictly adhere to in emergencies like this one, they were drummed into all firemen. Wait, plan and do not take risks! He knew all the procedures but they didn't stop him. There was someone in that car under that giant tree and they could still be alive, he wanted to reassure them that they were not alone and that people were working to get them free, the tree had settled and would not move again, he thought. Protect the public. The station manager was at the other end of the tree standing by the appliance, organising the crew but Matt had been drawn like a moth to the light, but what Matt didn't know was; the light had gone out.

Mavis stayed inside the house. Within minutes of her 999 call the street was awash with flashing lights and men in helmets and fluorescent all-in-ones, the roots of the upturned tree stood a couple of feet above the tall fireman who Mavis watched dropping down on to all fours to scramble under the massive trunk toward the beleaguered car, the young fireman was sure someone was inside the big car as its lights were still ablaze. The roots had decayed and weakened over many years of road and pavement works which combined with pollutants from cars and other poisons to attack the 250 year old Watchmen that Bexhill had grown up around for over two centuries. A final shove from storm Suzie finished the tree off. Tarmac, paving slabs and dirt had risen from the ground splaying like a filthy iceberg as the tree had rapidly descended towards the Shepstone's front lawn. Duncan Shepstone had departed by the time the first flashing vehicle had arrived and the rescuers would work that out later; while nursing the wounds of their own great loss.

Matt performed his crawl to the driver's door, which had crumpled into the ground when the tyres gave way and the suspension compressed, Matt had figured that the tree and the car were now fixed and immovable but the car still strained to resist the weight of the tree and its aluminium still had a few inches to give way to. Matt had just reached the driver's door hoping that there were no other passengers, it was plainly clear to anyone except to the chivalrous fireman that no doors would open, but Matt wasn't thinking about doors he just wanted to get a message of encouragement to the hapless occupant, he'd improvise. Unfortunately for Matt, Suzie and the tree didn't care for heroics, Shepstone or Matt. The fireman should have listened to his inner voice, he should have followed procedures and awaited instructions from his team, he realised this too late as Suzie picked up the tree one last time, what was left of the Jag's resistance finally gave way to the final crushing blow of the tree, the Jag gave way some more, just enough to stop a man on his belly from taking another breath. Although the gravy is getting thicker; the train keeps rolling on thanks to people driven by what they think is right, whose values don't allow for laziness or lack of compassion. This is what kept the few bad ones afloat. There was one less good one after this cruel and unforgiving evening.

Suzie was wreaking havoc and didn't spare the services that tried valiantly to help the public. Several more public servants were injured that night, along with a few members of the public they helped. One particularly stupid member of the public, thinking he was brave or daring had stood on a groyne at the ocean's edge with arms aloft, he was taken away by the sea, never to be seen again. People like him aren't necessarily a great loss to society, but a truly brave young man had lost his life trying to save the bin man of Bexhill. This why people honked their horns in support at the picket lines when the firemen were on strike. No one had the guts to say he was also a fool. Mavis looked on through the gloom and the leaves that scraped the living room window; as a kind, female police officer broke the spell and reassured her that everything that could be done was being done. Mavis offered her a chocolate finger and a cup of tea and told her, 'I think it's the brown bin on Tuesday'. She was right.

# CHAPTER 27

After the storm it was another warm, humid sunny day. The skinny Abyssinian walked around the bungalow looking up at the roof of Mrs Crick's home. This was the fifth or sixth time he'd done this daring walk over the last two days, always at a time when he thought the Black-Back would be atop the roof after its scavenging for food or killing of cats, but the big bird wasn't home and the mother wouldn't leave her brood alone for one skinny cat. Meanwhile, 20 other felines waited patiently, hidden in the thick foliage of the back garden, nestled in the conifers or waiting next door ready for the call to jump the fence. Others, the brave ones, even meandered in circuits around local roads and neighbours' gardens, apparently minding their own businesses but they were not, they were on red alert. A cat can sit at ease for hours by a mouse hole with every muscle in its body relaxed, until it senses movement or sound. It takes milliseconds for the muscles to contract and for the attack to begin. They were all nervous but they were also patient hunters and while their brains were on red alert, their muscles relaxed. These were the cats that Joseph had successfully used his powers of persuasion on.

The cats were all ready for an honest face to face fight, instead of being plucked up from behind and taken into space and they waited and waited, patiently for this fight to get started. The Abyssinian was obviously the bait and when the giant shadow fell across his back, the fur along the length of his spine automatically stood on end. He was scared for the first time in his life and didn't like the feeling - he took a cursory look over his shoulder. Any second now he expected to be airbourne but when he mustered the courage to crane his neck round and up for the second time, he saw the giant bird looking down from his perch, staring in wonderment at the beautiful skinny cat below.

The bird thought about landing and pecking the cat's face off, as he couldn't get his usual run up from behind, he'd lost the element of surprise but felt like killing again as he hadn't done so since the previous evening when he had drowned a small Persian. There was now a necessity for him to travel further afield for his kills as he'd noticed that the local cats were looking over their shoulders more and more, which is why he was away from home for extended periods, although he always tried to get back to his regular kill sites. This was a trap though and an alarm bell was sounding somewhere in that small brain of his but he ignored his instinct as, like Freddy; the wiring in his brain had become slightly rearranged by his obsessive behaviour, over-riding his natural intuition and decision making. Not that his decision making was ever that special, it was his massive presence that was usually what saved him. Nature had given him that advantage and he was about to throw it back in nature's face, which was a shame because he was in the prime of his life and nature had done a tremendous job in creating him. But nature has no feelings. The bird looked down at the cat and wanting to land and rip the Abyssinian's face off, there was something about him, that skinny blue cat, but he would never forget his first mistake when he took a cat on face to face. There was something about this one though and he wasn't prepared to take any chances against it, yet.

Joseph realised he'd made a mistake by taking that first tentative, nervous look over his shoulder. The bird had aborted the abduction as instinct kicked in and forced it to change trajectory and settle on its protective roof top. The moment a cat's head was not in alignment the bird's autopilot was disengaged and the conscious mind kicked back in and redirected him as self-preservation becomes key.

If a cat could curse itself, Joseph was doing that now but if he hadn't looked back he would surely have been airbourne by now, the stealthy cats that surrounded him would never have been able to thwart the attack. None of the cats could really know how expert the bird was at catching its prey, by the time they had jumped from their hiding places, Joseph would have been on his way to heaven followed by a bone crunching smack into tarmac or drowning at sea. Joseph and the cats didn't know it yet but Joseph's very first introduction to fear saved him and gave the cats a better opportunity to catch the bird, the bird now felt anger and frustration, emotions which dull common sense. He kept on staring at the skinny, blue cat that roamed, arrogantly around his property. The bird shuffled from side to side around the roof of the bungalow, looking at the cat and the sky and the cat and the sky, shouting into the air. He was angry. He was normally in charge, he called the shots but this cat threatened him and was disturbing the natural rhythm of his world.

Joseph sensed something in the air, he realised the plan wasn't working but seemed to know that all was not lost, he sat by the kerb side and looked up at the bird that had recovered from its tantrum and now stood stock still, only its feathers ruffling in the light and occasional breeze, the breeze that was left over from Suzie's angry outburst the night before, the bird's eyes were locked onto the cat. Joseph could not understand why, but felt he should scale the fence hidden by the Leylandii surrounding Mrs Crick's sanctuary. The fear in him grew as he entered the perfectly preened and pampered garden and as the fear grew so did the certainty that what he was doing would draw the bird down from his rostrum. As the bird shuffled his feet to follow the cat, the other cats converged, silently to the garden. The bird either didn't care about them or didn't notice them, he only had eyes for the Abyssinian, danger didn't register and unlike the cat, he still felt no fear, just a desire to introduce the cat to the sky which is where he looked to, to scream at his god again as the cat stalked towards the middle of the garden.

Dozens of unblinking pairs of eyes pursued Joseph, the composed and patient owners of which, waited expectantly. How could he provoke the bird into action? Joseph wondered. He noticed the water butt that Mega had once scaled and formed the same intention as Mega, to jump up onto the roof. The threat to the bird's family would surely entice a fight? Where Mega failed a clean jump to the roof, Joseph would succeed easily, he walked slowly towards the water butt without taking his eyes from the bird, leaping with no effort onto the top of it, the bird by this time had waddled with uncertainty down the slope of the tiled roof, craning its neck to see beneath the guttering to keep track of the threat, he began his hostile squawk at the cat again, the cat just sat down on the water butt with no acknowledgement of the bird; the cat weighed up its options by looking up at the bird, measuring the distance from water butt to guttering, then looking up at the bird again and then to the gutter once more, wriggling and appearing to prepare to leap from a seated started. But he couldn't jump because the bird was at the roof's edge. So the cat stopped to groom himself, licking his paws and coat, contemptuous of the bird's presence – one eye did not leave the bird, it gave the appearance of serene disdain, there was no serenity inside though, Joseph was terrified. However, the move elicited more and more anger from the bird, enticing him to fight. The deathly, shrill war cry grew in decibels as the bird stood in the shape of a letter T, feet planted on the roof's edge with its body rigid in a straight line across its legs parallel to the roof, its bill like an arrow trained at the cat and its rectrices fanned out behind pointing at the sky, his wings were spread to their full and majestic six feet which increased the fearsome spectacle. Joseph was scared but weighed the pros and cons of jumping onto the roof, for he knew that his compatriots would not get to join the fight before he faced this giant foe. He wasn't a fighter but figured he could hold the bird until his friends arrived to the contest; he couldn't jump onto the roof though because his route was blocked by the massive bird, he was relieved.

Nope, that wasn't the way. Joseph was too scared to face the bird alone on the roof, he jumped down and walked slowly back to the centre of the lawn where he could safely think of another plan to shock the bird into action, one less injurious to himself. Before he reached the centre of the garden, the bird pounced, pushing himself in an irrational attack from his perch at the edge of the tiles, propelling himself into an explosive dive at the cat. Joseph, aware of the flurry and whaling fury coming from behind began a sprint as if to escape from the garden; then stopped suddenly, then feigned left and then right, a moving target, he couldn't see the bird but what choice did he have? The bird couldn't hone in on the unpredictability of the cat's next move, and flailed in a frantic action to regain the air but the ground was getting closer. He over-shot the target, making an emergency landing into no man's land and turned to face the cat that was in between him and the bungalow. As the bird turned to face the hated little cat, so the other, hidden cats began to emerge from every angle to attack, sensing that this was their chance. Panic set in for the bird as it realised the danger, forgetting the cat in front of him, he tried to take off for the

143

safety of the roof again, directly in front of him. It seemed so far away.

He spread his great wings for one of the last times and began to run towards the bungalow but immediately found himself routed to the spot; five, six, seven cats pounced onto the wings latching on with their claws and teeth, angry and full of revenge. More and more cats piled onto the wings and back of the seagull who strained against the weight upon it, the weight that was getting heavier and heavier. The wings pumped to no avail. This is how it felt to have no control. The blind panic masked the pain from the dozens of claws hooked on to or slashing at its flesh, feathers left the bird to spread around the lawn. It was like the Chinese death by a thousand cuts, but less organised.

The cats' piercing, caterwauling screams, as are so often heard in the middle of the night through bedroom windows, when people are trying to sleep, increased to an almost deafening pitch. The cacophony could be heard throughout the whole estate and beyond. But this time it wasn't cat on cat it was cats on bird, one bird, and the cats thought it would be a lot easier than this, for although the bird didn't know it, they were clinging on for dear life. The cats' point of view was of a heaving mass of power beneath them and they were praying for backup which was arriving fast. The bird was soon invisible under the heaving mass of bodies of at least 20 cats. The mother seagull circled above crying, not daring to help. The brown freckled chicks watched on from the crook of the chimney stack. The mother cried on and on in the sky as she watched her husband dying on the ground. The blood began to soak into the manicured lawn. It was lucky Martin was coming tomorrow.

Domestic cats don't often eat their prey and besides, most of these cats had already eaten. For example; the ginger tabby in the fight with the giant bird had not long ago finished a *gourmet ocean gold pate with ocean fish* and the Persian with the knotted coat that had just lost his eye when the giant beak landed a lucky blow had recently polished off a *gourmet gold salmon and chicken in gravy* - the owners didn't take much notice of his coat, maybe they'd notice a missing eye, these meals didn't help with their speed and agility in the fight and they were now in a desperate hurry to get home to the commiseration of their owners and attention to their wounds.

Not many of the cats left the battle unscathed. The bird; although completely unaware of any of its successful wounding blows to a myriad of cats on the flight to its death, used every last scrap of its immense power to turn and peck and gouge at the cats in frantic and unpredictable stabs, pulling its wings in tightly, dislodging some of the cats, some falling in front of its mean, lacerating beak, which inflicted most of the pain. Mr Friedrich felt this pain, he'd sat bemused initially, under the

145

bench against the wall of the bungalow, then decided to join the fight, when he thought the bird was done for, going in to slash at the its head and eyes, but Mr Friedrich was rudely surprised and unprepared for the bird's second wind as the great head rose for the last time scoring among other injuries, a direct hit on one of Mr Friedrich's front legs, biting down hard, crushing bone. Mr Friedrich screamed and retreated back to his castle, as the bird slumped flat to the ground for the last time, all the energy sapped from its great body. The cats continued to rip and claw away at the bird until they were completely sure that there would be no more resistance. It was the vice like 'death grip' of one of the frantic cats, who in a panic and not by calculation had, by chance, managed to grab a hold around the bird's throat, that brought about the end of the gull's life. The battle lasted over ten painful minutes. The bird put up a good fight. As his vision began to blur and fade away, he was left with the images that were the silhouettes' of his children gathered together on the roof's edge to watch the end of their father's illustrious life. Did he have any regrets? It was unlikely that he did.


Joseph didn't take part in the slaughter, he sat and watched up until the point that he knew the bird was gone. Then he got up and walked home.

As the last of the fussy eaters sloped away from the scene, of pure carnage, the staccato sounds of the, not so fussy eaters began, the menaces' black and white heads popped from the hedgerows and gathered along the tops of the fences. They began by creeping nervously towards the stricken remains, fervently making their clacking sounds to elicit a response from the inanimate bloody object, wary too that there may still be cats around and respectful that what lay before them was the magnificent creature that they had all given way to so many times, before feasting on garden scraps. There was no life left in the seagull. The machine gun like clacking grew louder as other magpies arrived to enjoy the feast. They picked the corpse to the bone, enjoying every last morsel.

# CHAPTER 28

Edvard Munch's 'The Scream' was staring at the murder of Caesar – with feathers. The bird was invisible at times under a tidal wave of cat fur and tearing claws and blood. Channels of blood that hadn't soaked into the lawn flowed down between the gaps in the paving. Mrs Crick stood; frozen to the spot, behind the glass that framed her beautiful garden, eyes agog and mouth agape, in abject terror of what she was witnessing happen on her manicured lawn. She had been watching the sparrows one minute and then chaos erupted, 'Mr Friedrich? No.. No.. No... Mr Friedrich! No.. No.. No.. No! How could you Mr Friedrich?' she beseeched in a tremulous voice through the triple glazed windows that she had had installed after the sparrowhawk/pigeon incident, she grabbed the new window sill and held on tightly with white knuckled hands, unaware of the pain from her arthritis. The windows framed the action, it was as if she was watching a silent horror film, she tried to convince herself that it wasn't real. Run, run to the sanctuary of Sir Cliff Richard OBE, no stay, this is far too compelling. Tears streamed down her cheeks at the sight of the pure wickedness.

Mr Friedrich had managed, painfully, to pull himself through the floral decorated cat flap located in the new triple glazed kitchen door and was limping towards his owner's very loud and sad voice, which he figured was coming from the bedroom at the back of the bungalow, where she spent a lot of her time. The beak of the damn bird had held on to his front left paw so tightly and wrenched the leg from its attachment to the shoulder, snapping a bone, he was feeling the agony now that the adrenalin fuelled battle was making way for inflammation and pain. He needed the love and attention of his mum. He entered the bedroom and sat on the floor behind her as she stood stock still, staring through the window with her hands pressed firmly to her temples. Mr Friedrich attempted to lift his bad leg in the air and with a weak plaintive whimper he said: 'Meow'. But their relationship would never be the same again. Mr Friedrich never understood why.

Mrs Crick tolerated this pain, she knew life was cruel. Just because she hid from so many things now days, it did not mean that she was weak, her family tragedy was worse than this but resolve weakens with time and age and she just desired peace and quiet and harmony. Was that too much to ask? Unfortunately it is, for one can't control life, even if it's in one's own garden. This she knew. Martin was called to discard the remains of the Great Black-Back. He chucked it at his golf club and came back to wash and sweep away what was left of the blood and gore. She gave him a tenner and a tin of beer.

# CHAPTER 29

Katy loved working in Accident and Emergency because of all the gross things she got to see every day and she'd gotten a good look at Freddy's testes when the Doctor examined him, Freddy was in the position of a woman giving birth, to two coconuts, and still unconscious. She marvelled at the giant red and black scrotum and wanted a good feel, which she accomplished after the doctor had left the cubicle for a few minutes, the fear of getting caught added to the excitement. Katy was eighteen. Therefore, had technically become a paedophile but Freddy wouldn't didn't complain.

Freddy was moved to a private room once it was deemed that his injuries were not life threatening. Upon one of the nursing staff finding his phone among his things and ringing 'Home', it was discovered that the boy was only 14; the hospital acted upon its safeguarding policies and circumspectly called in the relevant local authorities. The case was cautiously pursued as suspected child abuse. The police were in trouble; again.

Freddy was never named as the cat killer because he was officially classed as a minor, therefore, his identity had to be protected by law, but he was sentenced to six months in a youth offenders unit which was suspended due to his balls injury and need for care. However, he was banned from owning any kind of animal for one year. Carrot was packed off to Freddy's grandmother who hadn't known Freddy since he was three, even though there were so few miles between them. Freddy only had sketchy memories of his gran. Carrot loved the new attention and quickly forgot about Freddy as Freddy forgot about Carrot. Carrot was replaced by Katy as Freddy's new play thing after he awoke one day in the hospital to find Katy's hand under the bed covers, copping a feel of the elephantine balls while looking nervously towards the door of the private room, she turned back to find Freddy's eyes wide open staring back at her, a smile cracking, wide across his face.

They would find that they had a lot in common over their four and a half month relationship, for Katy also liked PlayStation, horror and porn, she was sick like Freddy, probably even worse. They would spend hours playing against each other on the PlayStation and re-enacting scenes from porn on the internet. And Katy was particularly turned on by the fact that Freddy was the notorious cat murderer.  Four and a half months into the relationship though, feeling comfortable enough to be honest, Freddy admitted that he wasn't the cat killer, Katy left.

The cat killings were ended! Freddy's name would never enter the public domain. The press were banned from saying his name; he became just another unnamed youth offender, neither male nor female, just a thing that liked to kill cats. The family were too embarrassed about the crimes to press charges against the police for the assault, regardless of Freddy's incessant pleas of innocence, much to the annoyance of the child services' worker who was forced by her boss to keep everyone's dirty little secret. In today's modern world of transparency it's getting harder to brush things under the carpet; even with friends in high places, but whistleblowing although frequently in the media, is rare because people need to pay their bills and it's a scary thing for anyone to take the risk of coming up against the establishment; so the child services inspector involved in the case kept her mouth firmly shut. Although she did send appropriately worded emails and memos expressing her concerns, which she hoped, if the shit did eventually hit the fan, would absolve her of any wrong doing. She looked forward to the 'experts' on the news who were all blessed with hindsight, it was just a matter of time. The press love a good finger wagging, especially if there's a kid involved, then the blame game can really begin and heads can roll, who cares about cats when they can get someone strung up, especially if that someone is a social worker or other government person who gets exposed as negligent; more's the better. The media love a villain. It's never the fault of the evil sods who commit the crime because they probably had a bad upbringing – which was probably the governments fault too (cut backs) and more 'experts'. Expert after expert predicted the whole time that 'it' would happen at some point because they and the journalists who dug them up combined their collective wisdoms to predict it, and then the rest of the public got a chance to sit and finger wag too from the comfort of their armchairs. Franklin was scot-free. Freddy's brief brush with fame brought about on YouTube and Facebook would be as glamorous as his life would be.

# CHAPTER 30

The morning of the day after the death of Caesar the man and his dog passed the bungalow as usual, walking as they had been accustomed to, with their heads pointing in the opposite direction to where their bodies were going, the poo bag swung in circles, but on this occasion they looked more in curiosity at the bungalow's sloping roof, whereupon stood the mother gull and her three mottle brown fluffy babies, their heads bowed with eyes fixed upon something that could not be seen by the two friends passing by in the street beneath. The two friends still stepped up their pace the nearer they came to the twitten just in case of an attack. The four birds were not interested in the passers-by this time as they were all transfixed by an assembly in the bungalow's back garden, the mother gull gave only a cursory glance at the dog and its owner, as the two made their way to the sanctuary of the twitten.

Ground zero: Mrs Crick's garden, fifty seven cats gathered around the enclosed patch of land, some standing and some sitting, while some paced around in circles, all with one thing in common; fixed stares at the enemies on the roof. What were the cats all doing there? Babies are no threat are they? Joseph thought that they were and he had used his powers of persuasion one more time to bring the battle weary, unbroken, cats back to the murder scene. A few other cats had seen the procession on its journey and joined in out of sheer nosiness and now they all stared up to Mrs Crick's rooftop. Mr Friedrich elected to stay inside this time as he'd had enough of the stupid games and was still in pain. It took hours of plaintive meowing before Mrs Crick would take him to the vet, who had reset his damaged limb and put it in a cast at great expense to Mrs Crick. Mr Friedrich sat behind the safety of the kitchen door looking through the triple glazing at the cats in his garden. They were on his manor again but he didn't care this time. He was bruised and was feeling strangely out of place and unloved for the first time in his life as Mrs Crick's affections were now directed; no longer his way, but the way of her birds and a new replacement to Mr Friedrich, to a ginger usurper.

The birds on the roof had had enough of Bexhill-on-Sea and instinctively knew it was time to move on to pastures green, even before the second coming of the cats, which greatly helped to expedite the decision to move on. Of the three young birds, two stood roughly the same height but the third one the one that stood in the middle, between his two siblings, was taller and stronger and stared more intensely than its brother and sister. The mother was agitated and moved nervously to the highest point of the roof, deeply concerned for her brood of chicks. This was their first attempt to fly; if they failed they would die. She appealed to her children to come and join her with her usual ear drum shredding, high pitched call. The two smaller birds turned with a combination of a walk and a hop to join their mother at the roof's highest point but the big one stayed and stared, he stared at the blue cat in the centre of the garden with nothing but hatred in his beady eyes, he'd watched the cat's performance the previous day and what had happened to the big bird that protected him and his family for all of the young birds' lives. His mother cried some more and this time the noise penetrated through the strong stubborn skull, he took one last look at the skinny cat to embed its image permanently in his mind and then turned to join his family.

The mother kept talking and the babies listened, they were going to fly for the first time, she made certain that they were at the highest point of the roof. She took off from the edge, dropping maybe a foot or two before sweeping up above her children, crying all the time, bidding them to follow. They did, they tried. The biggest nudged his small, nervous siblings into empty space. The first one flapped for dear life mainly through fear, which would exhaust her quickly but for now it worked, she gained height, eyes locked on to her mother, guided by her cries, concentrating on flapping her wings that she'd stretched so regularly virtually on an hourly basis out of habit, so naturally. Something clicked the information is in the DNA, she understood how to fly and fly she did, not as gracefully as her mother, but well enough to take her out of harm's reach. The big brother then did the same with his other sibling, the weakest of the chicks who rarely stretched his wings, he hadn't felt the ache to stretch yet, unlike his brother and sister and was content to soak up the rays during the day and relax like his father, but unfortunately for him this innate laziness would cost. His big brother nudged him gently from the roof as he pushed backwards to resist against the force that was trying to help him to escape; he plummeted to the ground, no height was gained no air was collected by the frantic, hopeless uncoordinated flapping of the immature wings. The cats gathered up the baby gull that could not reach its mum. A clowder of marauding cats enveloped the luckless chick and enjoyed their wicked game, most were here for the fun of it anyway and they played with the squealing, bleeding chic on the ground for several interminable minutes.

'I don't believe it!' lamented Mrs Crick softly, upon returning from her customary early morning excursion to buy a *Daily Mail* from the local shop, why was this happening to her? A gaggle of screaming cats were pulling one of the baby seagulls apart that had been living on her roof for nearly six months, the baby was screaming in pain and flipping and squirming around the bloody pavement to avoid claws and teeth which were sinking into it with pernicious glee. It wasn't revenge but for the pure undiluted pleasure, the cats were enjoying their game, they liked to play and kill. The noise was deafening and gnawed through to Crick's disobedient nervous system which made her spine shiver uncontrollably, melting her heart, filling her with grief once again. She looked across the road to the pavement opposite, where a red metallic disabled buggy was parked with a fat pensioner sat staring opened mouthed, plumes of honey scented e-cig mist escaping her giant mouth and filling the sky, Darwin didn't like what he saw or heard, he sank lower into the buggy's basket and curled up with the *Daily Mail*, milk and lottery tickets to hide. Mrs Crick and the buggy were joined by a dozen or so more people, drawn out of their homes by the raucous screams of the cats and birds, many people preferred to stay indoors and peer through their net curtains, too afraid to leave the house.


Seagulls can live for 40 years this one only lived for six months. The big brother took flight easily, with no thought for the mechanics and technique of flying, it was the most natural thing in the world to him, he circled to take one more look down at his beleaguered brother, he knew he could not help, then he swept upwards overtaking his small sister barking encouragement at her as they headed for their sobbing mother, who had lost yet one more of her beloved family.

# Epilogue

Mrs Crick reflected on her life, at the beginning of the fantastic adventure that was marriage and motherhood; she had always dreamt of and looked forward to being a good wife and mother, and she was. But Mrs Crick never lived in denial like her daughter and son in law did. She had suffered grief and loss but stood up and dealt with it head on, although the disease and tragedy came as a bolt from the blue for her, she really had no other option than to deal with it head on, she became a long time carer and then a bereaving widow, with two bereaving children, then so quickly a bereaving mother when Manda developed the symptoms at age 35 but couldn't face what lay ahead of her. Manda had seen the horror first-hand, watching uselessly and painfully from the side-lines at the pitiful demise of her father whose symptoms appeared at age 45 and manifested so slowly; years of physiotherapy, speech & language therapy, various walking aids and adjustments to the house – a rail on every wall, a shower instead of a bath, all the paraphernalia from those dark days were still gathering dust in the garage, the council or whoever it was responsible, never came to pick it all up. And the frequent regular hospital visits took their toll on everyone. Manda took her own life at Beachy Head, a place that had claimed many victims. A beautiful place but that seemed to call to so many desperate and unhappy people. There was no element of surprise for the surviving daughter who did not have the disease and whose son was diagnosed with it, she was hurtling towards a brick wall at one hundred miles per hour, it loomed bigger and bigger, threatening her very sanity, she was losing her father, how could she face losing her son too? She couldn't. Mrs Crick didn't blame her daughter for wanting to close her eyes to the situation and keep them tightly shut. Mrs Crick never sat in judgement. But now separated by only two small miles Mrs Crick and her grandson were both isolated and alone.

Mrs Crick was to suffer again as she came home from the local shop only to witness another devastating scene unfold before her on the pavement beside her bungalow. A baby, why? She didn't know why, there was no 'why' but knowing that there was no 'why' didn't alleviate the pain she felt for herself and the bird that was dying in front of her. She didn't know it at the time, it seemed like a dream later on, but she ran into the melee kicking and shouting at the cats who, initially shocked by the mad pensioner interrupting their playtime, turned in retaliation but were quickly checked by the sight of a speeding buggy that had clattered down one kerb and up another bouncing uncontrollably behind Mrs Crick, barrelling straight at them, with yet another very angry pensioner whaling like a banshee, accompanied by a small dog yapping angrily from a basket on the front of the shiny red wagon. Darwin had cat friends but he'd just recently made a new feathered friend and although he was confused by this sight, he didn't like what he saw and was preparing to jump from the basket to help the old lady in her maniacal attack, she was kicking cats left right and centre, but the buggy was out of control and by the time Darwin could adjust to jump from the basket, the cats had scattered to the four winds. The buggy nearly flattened the poor bird, which wouldn't have been a bad thing as, by the time it arrived, there was just a dying bird left alone on the pavement. Darwin, his owner, Mrs Crick and the collective neighbours who had also closed in during the attack, looked on hopelessly. No one had the guts to put the poor bird out of its misery but Mrs Crick found the courage from somewhere to pick up the stricken animal, she held it in her arms and walked to the bungalow where the bird died. Mrs Crick and the neighbours watched the depleted family fly away with sorrow in their hearts. This time Martin buried the body of the bird at the bottom of Mrs Crick's garden, down by the shed. They stood by the grave for a while and she said a silent prayer in her head, she didn't believe in god; but there had to be something out there, didn't there? Superstition makes people do strange things but if it helps, it surely doesn't hurt, like the arnica she rubbed into the scratches on her lower legs, from the wounds that were her reward for an act of bravery, administered by several angry cats. Or the homeopathy she paid £30 a time for plus extras for sugar pills to treat her arthritis, which never improved but she swore by the magical remedy. Prince Charles can't be wrong!


The cats had all gone from Mrs Crick's garden and would not return again. The sparrows returned quickly though, in numbers, to pick at invisible things on the ground or on the stalks and leaves of the bushes and trees, the natural order was restored but there seemed to be an even more abundance of nature squeezed into the small garden this time. As was their wont to do, the sparrows peered at the other sparrows looking back at them through the mysterious, shiny, hard substance and tried to get at them by tapping their beaks gently against the slippery surface of the glass, Mrs Crick chuckled again and again in delight, she couldn't help it, as the tiny beaks scraped and quietly tapped the thick glass, she missed the tapping sounds though, the only drawback of triple glazing.

In another place far away from Bexhill the three seagulls flew west, resting occasionally when the smallest grew tired and needed to refuel or sleep. The big brown, mottled brother tried to appease its mother's pain but with no success, she was composed to an extent for she had to protect what was left of her family but she was hurting and her constant wailing reflected the inner turmoil she was feeling. The big chick was not tired, and stretching to its full height he was taller than his mother now, he looked east. One day, he thought, he would be going back to Bexhill-on-sea.

Mrs Crick sat in her secret place watching the sparrows in the foreground, thinking of the fresh grave at the bottom of the garden, forgetting about the cruelty. She had inherited a ginger cat as the owner, her grandson, was no longer allowed to possess him or indeed, come within 100 yards of any animal, not for one year, so said the law. He was the infamous cat killer terrorising Bexhill. Bexhill is a relatively small town after all. She would come to love Carrot more than Mr Friedrich. Carrot was a kind and loving cat that stayed indoors and wasn't interested in stalking other animals, he just craved affection from Mrs Crick which gave him unconditionally. And they both shared a love of sparrows and cuddles. Carrot and a cup of tea, dry tears making her face feel tight, and Cliff was on quietly in the background, making life good. Carrot liked Cliff too, remembering the thrash metal he was forced to endure before Freddy started wearing headphones. Freddy only really cuddled Carrot once and that was when Freddy's friends were taking a picture of them together. Just as Carrot had begun to purr and feel appreciated, Freddy threw him to the floor and virtually dropped kicked him out of the room. Carrot was purring loudly now, he got used to the hugs and Cliff very quickly. This was the life he dreamed about, he was finally happy. So Freddy was the cat killer? He was as bad as Mr Friedrich and his friends then! After the life Freddy had been forced to live, devoid of love, due to absent parenting it didn't surprise Mrs Crick that Freddy had lost the plot. She blamed it on the disease mainly but wondered at what ratio of blame was shared by the disease and the subsequent neglect by her derelict daughter and son-in-law in creating his cruel instincts.

# 10 YEARS LATER

Freddy's parents were still rich, they had focused on their careers and money and paid a hospice to take care of their son when the symptoms became too severe for Freddy to cope with on his own; they visited intermittently, never at the same time though. He sat on the floor most of the time, walking was a battle, he fought hard for every step, but he was never really a fighter and rested for hours on the floor of the home, mainly in the corridors listening to other peoples' radios. The symptoms kicked in properly around 25 years of age, stupid things like getting his knife and fork confused which made him angry. He smashed a lot of crockery plus his PlayStation and many other things before he entered the hospice. The parents replaced the PlayStation which he kept in his room but he was unable to operate it.

One day as he sat on the corridor floor, Freddy realised his foot was tapping away to *Mumford and Sons* as they chimed out of a hidden room somewhere, he wondered why he had wasted so much time listening to the stupid, insane crap that he used to listen to and wondered too at why he had hated this album when it had come out years ago but loved it now. He was beginning to realise that there were a lot of things that he had hated at the time, in the past, but that he was learning to appreciate more and more now as he sat on the corridor floors. Why was that? He never found an answer. He remembered a kind grey haired lady from his past who he thought was his grandmother, she spoiled him rotten and Cliff Richard was always on in the background. There was a gap behind the shed in her wonderful garden where he used to hide when the family played hide and seek. He realised now that the happy family just pretended that they couldn't find him and he chuckled to himself. They were his family, his grandmother, mother and father and maybe more, who were just a blur now. Why think about this? Because he never had time to before, he was plugged into angry howling music and a PlayStation and enjoyed the violence of killing people in a 'make-believe' world or watching violent porn played out by panting weirdos and Freddy was unloved. Poor Freddy, he should have watched the sparrows more. Now there was no time left. The newly promoted Chief Constable (CC) of East Sussex sat, tapping her foot to *Mumford and Sons* next to her son on the floor of the hospice's corridor. He didn't know she was there.

# THE END

16655577R00095

Printed in Poland
by Amazon Fulfillment
Poland Sp. z o.o., Wrocław